Dedalus Original Fiction in Paperback

Mensah

Gbontwi Anyetei, spent his infancy in Ghana, Nigeria,
Botswana and Zimbabwe before growing up in London.

He works in project management and in his spare time
he is an entrepreneur and keen blogger.

Mensah is his first novel.

Gbontwi Anyetei

Dedalus

ARTS COUNCIL
ENGLAND
Supported using public funding by

Published in the UK by Dedalus Limited,
24-26, St Judith's Lane, Sawtry, Cambs, PE28 5XE
email: info@dedalusbooks.com
www.dedalusbooks.com

ISBN printed book 978 1 910213 41 4
ISBN ebook 978 1 910213 59 9

Dedalus is distributed in the USA & Canada by SCB Distributors
15608 South New Century Drive, Gardena, CA 90248
email: info@scbdistributors.com   web: www.scbdistributors.com

Dedalus is distributed in Australia by Peribo Pty Ltd
58, Beaumont Road, Mount Kuring-gai, N.S.W. 2080
email: info@peribo.com.au

First published by Dedalus in 2017
Mensah copyright © Gbontwi Anyetei 2017

Printed and bound in Great Britain by Clays Ltd, St Ives plc
Typeset by Marie Lane

I'm supposed to die tonight

I pick the kettle out of the cupboard beneath the sink. It knocks my third gun to the floor. I use the handle of the teaspoon in the trigger-guard to return the gun to where it was and raise the kettle. I've lost my left sock, so I keep the bare foot off the cold stone tiles and I fold my arms as the kettle fills. The mobile phone I'm now ignoring rings, then stops.

ONE MISSED CALL... MERLEY

There's an episode of Columbo on the small soundless 14-inch screen TV which I keep in the kitchen. Out of the window I've got a captivating view of a flat that has an equally captivating view of mine. I'm very happy with the place. Sometimes when I come home from the rest of Hackney I almost feel like praying to God in thanks, but I don't, because I don't believe in God. I suppose I'm an atheist. But I'm an African and to be an African atheist is sacrilege.

On the TV there's a middle-aged woman killing a younger woman. I know she's not killing the younger woman because she's better looking. The older one's better looking. Maybe she doesn't know it. This must be the cover-up killing, because I've already seen Columbo on the screen. That's how I know the shiny classic TV show is Columbo and not Quincy, or the Rockford Files or the one with Perry Mason in a wheelchair. Columbo never turns up before the main murder has been committed. I always feel sorry for the victim of the cover-up kill because a lot of the time he or she didn't deserve it unlike the victim of the main murder. It's usually a blackmailer or inna witness, but sometimes it's just an unlucky mug in the wrong place at the wrong time. Columbo doesn't investigate the cover-up kill's murder in the same way. It doesn't eat at him like that first killing that brought him and his dusty car into the piece. At best their murder turns out to be just a clue for the main murder. You're dead and you're nothing but a clue. That's messed up.

ONE MISSED CALL... MERLEY

I switch channels. Local news without sound is even easier to figure out than an old cop show I've watched hundreds of times before. There's a police officer moving between street fixtures applying caution tape, and some of his colleagues standing around pointing things out to other police officers. It's east London and somebody is dead, violently, and they don't know who did it. Shaking my head I change back to the 70s murder and note that the water has almost – No! I can't go on like this. I've talked about what's on TV and now I'm about to start on about a boiling kettle.

Let me tell you what this is. I'm probably going to be killed soon, probably today. I don't expect you to save me. I'm betting you don't save lives. I'm going to send any evidence to lawyers, government officials, politicians, businessmen, some corrupt police officers, the police in general, and one doctor. Between them, they can variously expose, embarrass, jail or kill the men who kill me. If you're not one of the above, you've gotten this from someone who's in the know. Hopefully, they've already done something about what you're about to read.

I'm from a dangerous part of London called Hackney. I

know all the people in London that will put you in danger. Don't get me wrong, I don't know every gun-toter and knife hider by name, but the men they call boss, them I know.

There's not really a name for what I do. I've tried a few and had a few tried on me. A fixer, independent gangster, connection man. I make money by solving problems and resolving situations that you can't involve the government in. For every state of affairs that might get you in trouble if you talk to the wrong people – I'm the right man for you.

This is not what's going to kill me. It's a contributory factor at best. I do piss off important people in my work, it's inevitable, but then they'll owe a favour to someone who owes me a favour or who I'm safe with, so I get a pass, or a bly as they say on the road. They usually promise to kill me the next time, but by then I would've done more work, and more favours are owed. You get the picture.

Anyway, here's my problem: half an hour ago, I received a phone call from a man offering me some work. The man's name is Grayson Fielding, a man I don't know. Straightaway I'm worried. I've run an internet search on Grayson Fielding. It was a name I should be familiar with, but I wasn't before this morning. Grayson Fielding was educated at Marlborough College and Sandhurst before joining the Army. In his ten-year career he saw active service in the Falklands and the First Gulf War. He then went into the City working for a merchant bank. He is now on the board of four FTSE 100 companies and chairman of Investment Holdings which is owned by the Fielding family. He has a penthouse in the City, a house in Hampstead, an estate in Norfolk and property abroad. Men like Grayson Fielding with lords as friends and with millions of pounds – some of it in banks that are not offshore – don't have problems his government friends can't solve. This probably means nothing to you but to me that's Alarm 1.

When I was younger I used to read books about private detectives. Even with the law-breaking side to what I do, I'm the closest thing to a private detective I know. In literature the detective's job is to get set up. In detective fiction there is the noir prostitute. Disposable. The police are happy to have one less getting in their way and their deaths are not investigated that hard, whether or not they're the cover-up kill.

Three signs the detective has a target he can't see on his chest:

Alarm 1 – The job doesn't seem right. Why does the client need me at all?

Alarm 2 – A beautiful woman who the man can fall in love with brings him the work.

Alarm 3 – There's too much money being offered for the job.

In short, the more interesting a case appears, the more likely the case is not all it appears to be. Grayson Fielding's case ticks one box at least. The internet search turns up random images of the man but the ones that really get my attention are the ones of him with a young woman. His third wife, apparently. Maybe it was his beautiful wife who had the problem. Would a white man call in a Black man to solve his wife's problems though?

So if I know this path might get me killed, why would I choose to follow it? Well, the answer is, I don't know why I don't run. The fact is, I haven't been in real danger for a while. I miss it, I think. So I'm about to get some.

Oh, if this is going to work you'll be needing to know who I am. My name is Nathan Mensah. People call me Nate, because I can't get them to stop.

Weisse jungs bringen's nicht
TWO MISSED CALLS... MERLEY

Fielding rang me at eight o'clock in the morning. At eight o'clock I didn't know who Grayson Fielding was or his number, and I didn't know anybody who calls at eight o'clock, so I didn't pick up the call. I now replay the message he left.

'Hello, Mr Mensah. My name is Grayson Fielding. I was given your name and details as someone who should be able to help me with a... problem I have. Please call me back on...'

One can learn a lot from voicemails, and not just what people say and how they say it. That they leave a message at all and how they do it are informative. Fielding's tone is that of a man who's used to getting his calls returned. He left the message after calling me only once. This all tells me something. He leaves a pause between *a* and *problem*. I like that. It means what he has might just as easily be called a situation or misunderstanding. I excel in both.

Two-thirds of a cup of tea later I call him back. He picks up halfway through the third ring.

'Hello Mr Fielding. This is Nathan Mensah returning your call.'

'Mr Mensah, it's very good to hear from you.'

I'm straight to business, 'When will you be available to discuss your... problem?'

'Ten this morning, at my place in The Bishop's Avenue?' He doesn't wait for me to agree before informing me of the house number.

Grayson Fielding hasn't mentioned money but I've already priced him and the job. Seeing as this might be my last ever job I'm going to request half a million pounds but settle for a quarter.

Have no gun – will travel
ONE MISSED CALL... MERLEY

I've got a couple of things to do before my ten o'clock with Grayson Fielding. The first thing I've got to find out is if somebody wants me dead or if my name is doing the rounds today as a disposable brother. That's happened before.

I ignore the missed calls because I need to make one. I hold down the 2/abc touch button.

SPEED-DIALLING... KLU

I hear an explosion of glass just as I'm about to open my front door. I spring to the wall, put my back to it and listen. Holding my breath I don't hear more sounds of danger. Only more sounds of minor destruction. With caution I move my head towards a window which looks out at the road. There's a bunch of kids breaking into a car with the exuberance of youth. Four of them, all Black, none older than thirteen. One's done the breaking, two are looking out for the police and a fourth is standing astride his BMX bike screwing its seat back into place. Innovative but not original. It's the bike seat they've used to break the glass, bending it out of shape. They should have used one of those heavy D-locks. The car's a bright green convertible. If they'd all looked like they were doing it to feed themselves I would leave them to it, even if it did bring the police around. They just look bored though. The one who's broken the window now knocks loose bits of glass from around the opening so he won't cut himself as he puts his hand through it searching for the handle to open the door.

'Oi!' I open wide the large picture window I'm looking through with as much noise as I can, which is not much. 'Get away from my motor!'

All four of them stop what they're doing. They look around for a second before one by one they spot where my voice is coming from. We look at each other then BMX-boy looks at the two lookouts who in turn look at the biggest, the glass breaker – the operation's point man. He looks up at a Black man wearing a navy blue sweater under a fitted casual jacket. Suit and tie is my usual uniform but I don't want Fielding thinking I'm trying to impress him. The four juveniles are thus far not impressed.

'Get. Away. From. My. Car!' I repeat.

They all turn back to face me waiting for me to do something that should convince them to leave. I kiss my teeth and act as if I'm getting out of the window. Quick enough they assess that there's a good chance I can make the twelve foot jump down to the fake pebbles and be on them in seconds. Three run away laughing and putting their fingers up at me. BMX-boy cycles off and quickly overtakes the others.

'I know your faces! If I see you again, you're finished!' They now have a story to tell the rest of their friends. They don't look bored any more.

I watch as the slowest one disappears around a corner. After waiting a bit to make sure no one reappears, I get down and close the window and take the stairs to the ground.

The damaged convertible looks disappointed with the world. The removable top is a hard one or they would have gone in silently through the roof. I take a look. The driver's side window only has a few shards of glass remaining.

No east-London criminal would commit a daytime humble on a Thursday morning without running a risk-benefit analysis, and there's the benefit – a handbag lies just in sight under the passenger's side seat. There's a bunch of £20 notes inside it and a load of folded unopened bills still in their envelopes.

I've deprived those boys of quite a payday. £100 cash between the four of them wouldn't be bad for a minute's work. Plus, whatever they could get from any uncles who would use the utility bills for a spot of ID theft.

I bundle the handbag and everything else together including the car particulars from the glove compartment. There's also a blue docket holder holding an icon of a stick figure sitting on half a circle. It's only then I notice the car is parked in a disabled bay with the matching wheelchair icon. Even with the busted window it doesn't seem to belong in this bay. No kind of disabled person would drive an impractical coupé like this.

All the letters are addressed to a Kelja Tateossian. Number 48 in my building. That's my floor. I've got things to do with my time but in for a *pesewa*, in for a *cedi*. I return to my building and press the button of the flat on the opposite corner of my level. I think I hear a corresponding buzzing sound inside. I can hear the light footsteps on the wooden floor of a woman or juvenile male approaching. The footsteps stop. Either the corridor in front of the door is carpeted or the approaching person has stopped to look at me in their security monitor.

I try to adopt a pose like I'm not carrying a gun. I'm not carrying a gun so I should just stand still but I don't. I fidget and look suspicious. Still, the door creaks open part of the way. There's no, 'Who are you?' or 'What's your business here?' The door just opens like I'm not considered dangerous.

A man with one of those odd full beards with no moustache like Abraham Lincoln peeks through the door. He is very short and mixed-race Black or west Asian.

I address the beard, 'Is that your car downstairs? The green coupé parked in the disabled bay?'

He looks at me in the silence, not sure if he wants, needs or ought to answer my questions. The silence is broken by a grunt from the beard before a female voice beckons him back and the door is slammed shut. I hear a male and a female conferring. I wave the log book and papers in front of the door's spy hole and security camera.

The door opens again and the man's eyes watch the items pass in the gap.

'My car!' says the woman behind him. Her eyes are the same green as the car.

'The Fiat?' I add.

'Yes!'

I'm suspicious, because beard contradicts her, 'It's a Peugeot!'

That's all I need and I'm happy to hand over all the particulars I'm holding, but before getting on with my day I am curious whether this odd couple can keep the pantomime up.

'You got any brief?'

Silence.

'ID? Identification?' I add to un-confuse her, or both of them.

Immediately, a skinny tanned arm that doesn't belong to the beard twists out of the opening, and I stare at the side of her wrist to the base of her palm. Tattooed in calligraphic letters is the name *KELJA*.

'I see,' I say and because I have to maintain positive relations with my neighbours I shove the paperwork in the pocketbook and I hand the tattooed arm it's property. If it's not theirs they have gone to a lot of trouble to steal an identity, even with the French-Italian car discrepancy. The hand disappears with its property into the apartment then comes back empty requesting a handshake.

Bemused I grant it, asking, 'If you're with the AA or something, call them to come fix your car window! Kids broke into it. I saw what happened from my flat and disturbed them before they got anything.'

'Oh! Thank you!' The beard's voice this time.

'Welcome to Hackney: where your property is all our property!' I muse loudly and mostly to myself as I descend the staircase.

SPEED-DIALLING... KLU

Still no response.

I leave a message.

'KLU. MENSAH. CALL ME.'

Grayson Fielding and the stage show I've just left behind mean I am more occupied with my thoughts than normal, so I see them too late. A familiar man and an unfamiliar woman. They weren't in uniform but with their dark, loose three-quarter-length coats they might just as well have been.

I didn't need this. I slow down then stop walking but too late, I'm thinking. I lift my right foot to take a step back. I manage the step back. I can't believe I haven't been spotted. One and a half more steps and I could turn, put my collar up and actually make it out of here. I could pretend not to hear if they call me back. Still holding my breath I shift my body weight ready to take another step. Then, the pathetic Peugeot's alarm starts blaring. I swear under my breath. As both people turn in my direction I can no longer lie to myself into thinking I could have got out of here without being seen.

The man blinks at me with a curious expression on his face. The longer he does this the longer the debate raging in me continues. If he can't recall my name after all this time, it's a humbling experience for me. If he can remember but is trying to intimidate me, he's humbled himself. He changes tack and smiles. He looks at the shining Peugeot and the noise it is making about a hundred metres back, then at me, while I try to look like I'm not involved. His build and his cauliflower ears are evidence of a boxing past he could blame most of his ugliness on. He still forces his fat into muscle at the free-to-use station gym but the slow deliberate way he talks is a better sign of his fighting past than his physique. Here's a man who for several reasons doesn't have to rely on eloquence to...

'Mensah isn't it?'

'Inspector Roacher,' I say by way of hello and how are you?

Roacher puts an arm out towards his partner. His arm matches the direction of the Navarino Road sign above him affecting an invisible boundary. 'This is Detective Inspector George.'

Detective Inspector George bears a striking resemblance to my old foster mother. She's about forty years her junior but easily her equal in obesity. Set in her much smoother face are eyes that don't have the love for me that Aunty Merley's eyes have. D. I. George could have been anything: a teacher, politician, a chef, but she has chosen to be a police officer even though she hasn't that hardness in the eye women police officers always have that tell of all the bullshit they take from their male colleagues and how they'll be damned if they take any from other men.

Roacher turns to his colleague, 'Oh, have you met Mr Mensah?'

'Mensah?' she asks.

'Yes, Mensah like the brain club but with an h!' Roacher shows his open mouth to us with a lot of British bulldog teeth in it, 'Mensah, Nathan, also known as Nate.' Roacher taps the signpost behind him like he's sending a message in Morse code, 'We've had him in a few times for questioning... but no convictions.'

The car alarm finally stops then.

17

Roacher takes to squinting at me now, 'Nate, for the benefit of my new colleague, how is it we haven't managed to get you locked up?'

There's silence. Roacher looks at me. He actually wants an answer.

'Because I didn't do it.' I reflect.

'Didn't do…?' Roacher urges.

'I didn't do… the things that the Metropolitan Constabulary come around asking about, and locking people up for… It wasn't me.'

'Well, there you have it!' Roacher comments for Detective Inspector George's benefit.

His voice gets accusatory for the first time, an impressive delay for this police officer, 'What about the things the Constabulary,' he rolls this word around his mouth before continuing with his sentence, 'can't prove? The facilitations? The ideas? The introductions? The tip-offs? The information?'

I think about shrugging but don't.

'D. I. George is very well educated Nate, just like you! Miss George tell Nate here what qualifications you hold.'

When he uses an unmarried title instead of her police one, I hope for a scowl or rolling of the eyes but she holds the thin blue line. The police I've met are always too professional to let personal dislikes of colleagues show in front of career criminals. I have to find other weak traits and responses to exploit. A fat Black policewoman should have her share. Meanwhile D. I. George informs me, 'I hold a degree in sociology and anthropology and a masters in criminal psychology.'

In a voice that sounds like he's sulking Roacher says, 'Policing is just like any other industry going through evolutionary changes. We started with the thief-takers, and the glorified errand boys for the upper classes, then came police officers like me who share the same background as the criminals we're trying to catch.' He pauses, contemplating D. I. George. She has nothing to add. He respects this. 'Now, we've got the community police fad with officers attending partnership meetings with social workers and ambulance drivers and all sorts, trying to figure out how to hug infant criminals more. But see, criminals are getting smarter so we have to keep up. We have to develop a new way to cope with the modern gangster.'

ONE MISSED CALL... MERLEY

'Very soon D. I. George here and a merry band of highly-educated officers will make it their life's work to target that whole grey area of the underworld you operate in.' Roacher looks at me. 'You Nate, are what this new police force is calling... What was it again?'

'An enabling factor.' George fills in.

'An enabling factor!' Roacher echoes, 'Yes that was it. An enabling factor.' Our meeting was almost over now. 'So as you go about your business today I want you to keep that in mind, alright?'

Silence.

I use body language to say I would like to leave now, but say, 'I'll keep that in mind.'

He doesn't nod. He just looks at me and his eyes seem to get glassier by the second.

I walk on past them not looking back. I know he won't still be watching me, but maybe she is. Roacher has always been a policeman that didn't take his job too seriously but I don't know what the addition of this educated partner and that bizarre breakfast conversation mean for me.

Still, I'm happy I left my guns at home.

Possession of a firearm without a certificate
Firearms Act 1968, section 1
Maximum Penalty: Ten years imprisonment per count and
an unlimited fine.

I'm relieved when I turn the corner and inside a minute I'm under the railway arches where I keep my car. Nonchalantly I take a look behind me checking again that I haven't been followed.

I crouch by the metal garage door shutter. I turn the key in the lock that's at the lowest possible point of the door. My index and swearing finger scrape the filthy ground. I hate this part. I hear a thick, greasy unlocking sound that corresponds with the key feeling light in my hand. I stand, bringing up the garage door. Waiting for me on the other side is a clean business-blue saloon car. I point a remote at it and six lights blink twice at me making the car look even more glorious in the gloom of the otherwise empty breeze-block garage. I like this part.

'No one from our tribe drives a fancy car like this! You must be doing alright for yourself!'

I sit in the car's right-hand tan leather seat and select some orchestral music before I move it out.

Hackney.

There's nothing like playing classical music at the beginning of a serious working day. Under old shop fronts of yellows and reds some joyless men in council green scrape at the purples and pinks of illegal flyers and posters, that used to be the work of Black boys wearing white on community service. The various shades of grey of east London's roads and pavements are monitored by a blue sky. It is turning into a decent day by London standards.

I pass the eyesore that is the derelict Chimes Night Club with its Palace Pavilion annexe. None of the Olympic money that Homerton and Dalston were seeing has found its way here. This was the scene of real trouble back when it was open and only slightly less now its crumbling. For a lot of bad men, it holds a special place as the starting line for Hackney's murder mile. Some say the nineties war zone had been brought about by drug tsars manipulating the local boys in their employ. Others say it was down to the Yardies, or the Tottenham boys fighting the Haringey boys, a spill-over from old prison feuds. There are those who maintain it was never as bad as all that and was just police looking to beef up their arrest figures by rounding-up the usual suspects. Nobody could say for sure, including the victims who had survived, and especially boys who did the shooting. It was probably all the reasons people gave and more.

What made the nightclubs and this corner in particular the ideal place for trouble was the Leabridge Roundabout I am driving around. From this small hub a driver or biker who is handy with the steering and the pedals could take the first exit and be in Islington within five minutes. The second exit would get you through Upper Clapton and into Haringey in three minutes and the third to Waltham Forest in sixty seconds. Real adventurers would ignore the roundabout completely and opt for an eight to ten minute chase to Tower Hamlets or Newham, depending on whether you take a left or right at Hackney Wick. Swift access to five different boroughs.

SPEED-DIALLING... KLU

No response again.

Mobile telephone, use of while driving
Road Vehicles (Construction & Use) (Amendment) (No 4)
Regulation 2003, No 2695
Maximum penalty: £1000 fine for conviction in court or £100
fixed penalty notice.

Here there are three religious buildings within a stone's throw of each other. A synagogue off the roundabout's northernmost shoulder, a methodist church south-east of the junction and a mosque to its west. Opposite the old synagogue I mount the kerb and turn off the engine.

I leave a message again.

'CALL ME IN THE NEXT FIVE MINUTES OR DON'T BOTHER.'

I shake my head, but I know what I'm going to have to do, just like I've always known.

Impatient, I sit in my car parked slightly uphill pointing north directly beside the big brown brick and ultra-white windowsills of the Downs Estate. It is a quiet Thursday morning, so only one jogger complains through the windscreen about my car being parked on the pavement blocking his path. I stick two fingers up at him.

Jumping out, I hit the remote lock almost before my door is closed and again there's that silent flash of all lights to tell me it would take a good car thief at least three whole minutes to get in and try and drive it away instead of the usual thirty seconds.

I scan the deceptively quiet-looking estate. I love the name of this particular block. Moredown House. More down, is this as down as it gets?

In the stairway marked with graffiti, urine and bleach, I forgo the lift, taking the steps three at a time I'm up the two flights in a dozen bounds. It's a familiar pattern. Like my own place the flat I'm looking for is on the first floor. I walk along the outlying passageway running my finger on the low wall until I see bird shit. I stop at the second door and flick the letterbox flap between thumb and forefinger so that it opens and shuts twice in quick succession. It's louder than a post delivery but not ominous enough for the bailiffs. In the long silence that follows I wait admiring the dissonant exhibit of homeland flags hanging out of windows. There is not a lot of red, no white, and little blue on display but there are green, yellow and black in abundance.

Someone moves towards the door fast. This means it's not who I'm looking for. I hear the rattle and squeaks of children's toys being kicked as a woman opens the door.

'Alright Letitia?'

'Hello Nate.' She screws her face up, and her eyes of bristling brown fire at me.

'Is he in?' I ask, clearing my throat.

Pausing, she looks at me with open suspicion and hostility.

'What makes you think he's here?'

I look away. He is here.

'Are you coming in?' she dares.

'Nah, you're alright, I...'

She closes the door in my face, quietly but firmly because slamming it would hurt her more than it would me. I look around to mark what has changed during our conversation. Nothing has. It is still a council estate in the centre of Hackney and I make to leave it. Letitia makes me nervous. She is a hard-working woman. I am always uncomfortable around genuine hard workers. She isn't the only one around here but most of the people in this estate that worked preferred jobs they could leave for at night so concerned public citizens do not make calls that stop their unemployment cheque from arriving.

I return to my car and take my seat. Letitia's flat is the only one with blinds and not boring patterned lace nets like all the others. Even the empty flat below and its squatter-proof steel-window barriers can't reduce Letitia's flat's standing as a cut above the rest.

Unconsciously I select the radio instead of the MP3.

'The police are appealing for witnesses to the killing of a woman whose body was discovered in the early hours of this morning in east London, in the Brownswood area of Hackney. The woman is described as from eastern Europe, in her mid to late twenties. The police investigation into the killing of the woman...'

Letitia's window opens noisily with blinds clattering against each other. I kill the radio. A head sporting brand-new plaited cornrows appears at the window. Hand and arms follow pushing the blinds to give space for a torso and a partial rear end that rests on the window. I wince as the blinds become a tangle of light wood and string. Letitia is going to be pissed off. The man yawns, covering his mouth although there's no one to impress. Yawn incomplete he brings his hand down and goes back to preparing a stick of what I have every reason to assume is marijuana. Licking his lips he nods at me.

I nod back. 'Klu!'

He nods back, 'Wassup man?' This is Klu. Klu is a Black man five years younger than me but more muscular, smaller than me and shorter tempered. Klu is a criminal but unlike me he doesn't have the patience for some of the stuff I handle, so he's fond of the easy shit. He watches my back when I need it, and I watch his back all the time.

I throw my hand up in an everything and nothing gesture. 'I've been calling you!' Klu squints at me. Between us is a stretch of grass and weeds around a big hole in the ground that used to be a bomb shelter. Trying to figure out how low we can talk and still hear each other is a game we've played for years.

'Yeah. You've been calling.' He thinks about this fact that both of us hold as clear and self-evident. He could make excuses or lie, but doesn't have the energy, and there isn't anyone around to impress. He settles for abbreviating the question he began with, 'Sup man?'

'Let's go.'

'For what?' Klu frowns.

'A drive,' I answer.

Klu doesn't relish the idea but his frown clears as his bleary eyes seem to notice the car I'm in for the first time and he exclaims, 'Jheeze! What did you do with your Black-Man's Wheels?'

'Had to change it up,' I shrug.

'Aight fukkit, I'm coming!' Klu says disappearing into the room attached to the window. I turn the sound back up on the radio but the news report has finished.

Grayson Fielding, an attempted break-in of a car outside my drum and an angry Letitia. The omens say this isn't going to be a good day. I feel guilty for bringing Klu in on it. I do know other people. People with more back-up, power and guns. Some of them possibly even smarter than me, like Grayson Fielding might be. None of them are better than having Klu around though.

This is a neighbourhood – this ain't no residential district!

Klu adjusts his trousers to the usual level below his waist. He has perfected the balance between swagger and cautious awareness of possible predators. He looks back at his flat and then left at the rest of the world.

'Seen!' Klu grins at me and admires my car. He makes an o-shape with his mouth, 'Don't see a brother during a six-to-twelve-months stretch and he goes all big-time executive on me! This is some shit! "You can't arrest me! I've got that diplomatic impunity shit!" '

There will be a few more minutes of this and I've allowed for that. Through the mirrors I watch as Klu sits on the boot and does some kind of dance. I feel a gentle and unhurried rocking of the car.

When he finally returns to within my normal peripheral vision, I ask Klu, 'You coming or not?'

'Definitely! I'm going to sit in the back so people think you're just chauffeuring me in this muthafucka!'

I would object but it wouldn't be a bad idea for where we are going.

When he's in behind me, he beat-boxes a reggae rhythm and pointing forward like Kwame Nkrumah, sings like Buju Banton, 'Driver! Don't stop at all!'

'Oh – who's gonna look after Addy?' I interrupt, turning on the ignition.

'Letitia's got it!' Klu decides before carrying on with his interrupted mimic.

Just as I pull away I can hear Letitia's voice calling out, 'Klu, where are you going without your son?'

Klu slaps the back of my seat urging me forward and still singing drowns out Letitia's insults that no doubt follow us along Downs Park Road. Klu is a troublesome guy. His girlfriend and his mum blame me for most of the trouble he gets into. Maybe they are right. Because of this, his girlfriend doesn't like seeing me, and his mum likes to see me too much.

Klu's crooning isn't half bad but I'm glad he stops when he

can't remember the remaining lines to his song. It's my turn to annoy him by putting the orchestral music back on, loud.

I drive fast down Queensbridge Road. I reach fifty miles an hour on a road with a thirty mile an hour speed limit. Klu howls with ecstasy as a speed camera flashes in my wake.

Failure to comply with traffic signs and speeding
Maximum Penalty: A fine and three points on licence
Road Traffic Regulation Act 1984, section 89

I like to set those off every so often. Right now a crime is being committed somewhere that the police might like to attribute to me except for my image being caught by these speed cameras.

Vehicle licence/registration fraud
Maximum Penalty: 2 years imprisonment and/or £5000 fine
Vehicle Excise and Registration Act 1994, section 44

We stop at the traffic lights at the corner of Clarence Road and Lower Clapton Road. A short Black man looks my way. His fat arms are folded over a lumberjack check shirt. His jeans have the same painted symbol as the one emblazoned on the baggy T-shirts Klu likes wearing. I'm sure he's looking at me despite the big sunglasses he has on. He looks me up and down like women look at other women in clubs. Darker skinned than Klu and I combined, his scalp and beard are fully shaved and tended.

'Togolese Mike,' Klu tells me the man's name. 'He's always watching, man's like a fucking traffic warden!'

'You talked to him before?' The traffic lights move us on so I can stop watching. Togolese Mike watches us, 'What's he saying?'

'Who cares fam?' Klu kisses his teeth, 'I don't even think my man's from east London! He might be from south or anywhere! They say he fences a bit and shoots some weed and them little man tings there. I see him yesterday, now today... He's looking at us man all hard and shit!'

'Maybe he used to be a traffic warden?' I suggest.

'He's getting ghosted soon bluhd – trust me!' Klu says.

'So this guy's already got a target on his forehead just cos he's from out of the manor?'

'Might do that shit maself! How's man just turn up and start shottin'? He ain't paid his dues or nothing! We've got to protect our postcodes. E5! E8! Shit is real!'

I look at my watch. I've got a few minutes. I turn the car round so I face the opposite direction. We head into residential roads minding their own business, lined with two-storey terraced houses with either garages, gardens or basements. Once upon a time the residents would have fought over house prices. Now the residents are just happy to live in an ever-expanding part of Hackney where ambulances and police cars rarely visit.

About a minute after weaving through it all, I stop the car and point out an old forgotten road sign to Klu. The sign is not as big as the new ones with London Borough of... It was a slender and beaten old label on the side of the house that simply read Saratoga Road NE.

'NE? What's that mean?' Klu asks the question I want him to.

'It means all these NEs used to be North East London.'

'For real?'

'Yeah. You never thought about how there's a South East postcode, South West and North West but there's no North East? How round here it's just a North and an East?'

Klu frowns again. He hadn't thought about how Hackney wasn't NE, and how this was only because people in Newcastle needed to get post too.

'Klu, if you're going to kill somebody, kill them for something real. Years ago, Stoke Newington was its own borough and Shoreditch too. Somebody comes along and says alright – all you three come under Hackney. Now, you're talking about taking lives because of the pen stroke of some Royal Mail joker!'

Klu got stubborn again, 'Mate! Don't matter what we fight over. We're warriors and so we're ready when the real war starts. We lead from the back nigga!'

I shake my head at him, and put the car through the gears. While I sounded like a mix of youth worker and local TV documentary short, Klu doesn't. 'What do you give a fuck anyway? You ain't out on the road like the rest of us so why should you give a shit when one of us falls?'

Klu makes small talk. I always like to let people talk for a minute. I learn all kinds of interesting things and sometimes get answers to questions I'm too polite to ask, or I would have forgotten to ask, or would never have thought to ask.

'You heard about the two girls that died last night?' Klu asks.

This was an obvious example. Our kind of small talk, 'No. Where was this?'

'In Brownswood.'

'Oh.' I think back to the news report from this morning, 'I heard about one.'

Klu nods, 'There was one but they just found another body near that one, Letitia was watching the news as I left. So now it's two. The first body was on the street like any random pigeon, the second girl's body was in a house like...'

He can't think of what animal get's killed in its own home. That would be humans.

'The police will want this one!' Klu predicts.

'Who do you think they were?' I ask the underworld pundit.

'Who knows? Maybe they're just pretty so the media will love them. Or if they're not pretty they're suckin' someone that's fuckin' someone that means something in this London town.'

Klu's news about the two girls is definitely something to think about but I still have more immediate concerns. 'Anyone been asking around for me in the last day or so?'

'I've only been out the last day or so!' Klu's default frown is back, almost as if he's disappointed not to be talking about dead women any more. 'For you, the great Nathan Mensah? Somebody wants you, they find you innit!'

He was right. Grayson Fielding did. But how?

Klu leans over and scrolls through the music in my MP3 library.

Annoyed I ask, 'I thought the rule was, "Never touch a Black man's radio".'

Klu winces at the piano solo that plays. 'That don't count when the Black man is playing white boy music!'

'That's Samuel Coleridge Taylor man.' I stop at a zebra crossing for an old lady passing. 'He was Black.'

'Don't f...' Klu inspects the song information as it scrolls past on the car's music system display: "1897 production date of *Othello Suite*". 'For real?!'

I look at him in the affirmative. Klu takes out his phone and checks on the internet if I'm telling him some not-for-profit lies. The old lady in front walks excessively slowly, with an extreme limp that looks as if it's for some insurance investigator's benefit. I try to relax. If there was a known threat against me Klu knew of, I would know by now. There's definitely a chance this Grayson Fielding job isn't as dangerous as all that. I've had customers with unusual cases before. I've even had regular cases from unusual customers. The old lady finally passes the front of the car so I can carry on without hitting her.

'See, that's what I mean!' Klu has discovered I wasn't lying 'Everything they do they took from us. Get me?'

'Ok,' I follow.

He reads something he doesn't like. 'He was from Croydon though? He was from the south?' Klu is leaning over cutting off the track and replacing it with Kano. This time with some ugly gymnastics Klu reseats himself in the front passenger seat next to me.

'So wassup?' Klu thumbs back the way we had come and the question I asked back there. 'Who's calling for you?'

'Nah, nobody!' I reply. 'Just standard watching of my back bro! The sort of thing you should be doing.'

Klu nods slowly, believing. 'Two dead white girls.' He whistles with a kind of concern. 'Even boys in the bin will be getting a pull to find out what they know about who sold a gun to whom and where and why and when.'

I lazily pull over into a three-car-length runway of a parking space and smile at Klu. I use my gear-changing hand to push him friendly like but hard into the side door, 'I'm glad you're out. Damn, have you gotten bigger?'

'Nothing to do inside apart from reading and lifting right?' Klu nods, flexes his new muscles casually, then he also asks me something he suddenly remembers, 'Have you seen Dedei lately?'

'Nawh,' I shake my head. 'You seen her since you got out?'

'Nawh, she's in Milton Keynes. Coming back today.'

He stops.

'She didn't come visit me y'knaa. Said she couldn't. Just

on the phone a lot. She calls me – I call her, knawmean? She tried to visit me once but she couldn't… just kept crying. Felt guilty y'knaa.'

Quietly, I stare at my hands that I have placed on the steering wheel and mutter what I've been muttering for all of Klu's 6–12 month sentence. 'I didn't know man. You should have called me!'

'What for?' Klu spits, 'Dedei's my sister! Tony hits my sister and I'm supposed to come to you for help or permission to go after him?'

'That's not what I'm saying,' I lick my lips.

Klu sighs loudly, 'You hear anything from Cromber's people?'

'No,' I shake my head confirming what Klu already knows.

'Neither has anybody else!' Klu's voice expresses his surprise that Tony's crew weren't promising recriminations for Klu bloodying one of their lieutenants.

'The guy hit your sister. Cromber won't do a thing.' I reassure him without sounding like I was reassuring him.

'And what, they ain't gonna come at Nate Mensah's cousin, eh?' Klu balls his hand into a fist cupping it with the other.

'It's not that,' I say shaking my head again. 'Cromber and his guys don't even like me. It's just the way it is. There are some rules out here still! Tony didn't even make a statement to the police, or come to court, did he? It was that police officer's affidavit that caught you out.'

Klu kisses his teeth, then raises his head at me, 'They say he ain't been around no more?'

'That officer or Tony?' I ask.

'Tony!' Klu states but looks unsure of himself, as if he's just missed out on a more interesting question.

I reply, 'I ain't seen him around for months, that stomping

you gave him must've worked a treat.'

Klu looks at me hard the way he did before, then he sniffs piously, 'If they wanna bring it, they can bring it! I'm here innit. This is me!' Klu skips to the next music track for something to do while he talks.

'If it had been you... you wouldn't have got caught, eh?'

'It's not that you do these things, it's just how you do it... all those witnesses... right in the middle of Sainsbury's...'

I'm done talking but he interrupts me anyway, 'Look, yeah! You do your Keyser Soze leave-no-trace thing, but sometimes man's got to... you know?' Klu wills me to understand, 'He put hands on my blood!'

I nod. I did understand I suppose.

Silence.

Klu spits, 'I told Dei not to mess with Nigerians!'

'Tony was from Malawi,' I say and before Klu can shrug and say what's the difference, I continue, 'So if you had the chance you'd do the same again?'

'Definitely.'

More silence.

'At least you didn't spark the pig who broke up the fight.' I reason into the void, 'He wasn't even real five-oh. One of them pay-as-you-go-popos. He stopped the fight while his bitch partner called the real police.'

Before another silence can take hold my phone rings.

THREE MISSED CALLS... MERLEY

I shake my head at the screen, 'It's your mum.' I raise an eyebrow at Klu. 'She's probably calling to make sure I do a better job of looking out for you. Tell her I'll call her back.'

'I'm not telling her nothing!' Klu shakes his head, 'You know how she takes bad news personally.'

'Yeah well,' I tap on the steering wheel, 'I've got somewhere else to be.'

'I thought me and you were rolling today?' Klu asks loudly.

'Maybe later.' I point at the building we're parked beside, where only Klu would be rolling.

Klu makes a petulant sound as he looks at the probation service area office. 'Those guys say I need to come here something like 11.00 am, 11.30 am, 12.00 pm.'

'Something like… "11.00 am, 11.30 am, 12.00 pm," huh?' I repeat with patience. 'What time is it now?'

Klu shrugs.

'So go now, they won't mind.' I tell him.

Klu exhales loudly. I look at my watch. Fielding's waiting for me by now. I've got thirty minutes to get there.

'Klu, you just need to be another guy on parole that they see. So when laws start getting broken hereabouts you won't be the troublesome one that jumps out from their lists, when the police come asking for names of a nigga to fuck with.'

'What? We gonna be breaking the law and shit?'

'Today? Almost definitely!' I reassure him openly.

Klu smiles the widest I've seen him do in three months. Cromber and his people are forgotten, for now. Holding a hand over his mouth to obscure his voice he speaks in an American accent despatch-radio style. 'APB! I repeat this is an 'All Points Bulletin' for a well-dressed IC3 male in a knight in shiny armour blue German town-car. Caution. He's unarmed but dangerous anyway.'

'Wanker!' I smile. 'In America they don't use IC3 business. They would just say Black or number one male.'

'They're both what you iz!' Klu points at me with mock deference.

'I met a policewoman that looks like her today, your mum.'

'Yeah?' Klu asks, genuinely curious and happy not to be

talking to a probation officer right now. 'Was she friendlier than my mum?'

'I don't know yet. Probably not,' I start the engine. 'I'll catch up with you in a couple.'

Klu exhales, he jumps out of the car and pulls his hood up over his head. He's already annoyed with me, so I won't hang around to make sure he goes in. But I move forward a couple of car lengths before I remember something, then reverse back again. My memory was all over this place this morning. 'Klu, shout me if you find out what the streets are saying about these dead women.'

'For real!' Klu says. We both realise today is not going to be good day for any of Hackney's operators, whatever their level. The dead women's problems are over, and mine are about to start.

Expensive Shit

I expected the house where I had to meet Fielding would be one that came with grounds I had to circle. Instead I find a row of big houses. The biggest house must be Fielding's because it excites my satellite navigation system the most. It has an intercom mounted on a fancy bollard at the end of the driveway. I push the button in the centre of it.

A few seconds after, a cold voice asks a static diminished question that I translate as a request to state my business.

'Mensah to see Fielding.' I speak into the grille in my best public school English.

I follow the drive uphill towards the house and instead of seeing a Rolls Royce or Daimler parked there I'm surprised to see a helicopter. The front door of mostly opaque glass opens as I approach. A tall well-built security man nods in greeting.

'Mr Mensah, this way please.'

I follow him along a passage and up a staircase. He knocks on the third door on the right, then opens it. 'Mr Fielding is waiting for you,' he says before departing.

It's a study-cum-office where I see a man looking out of the window, his back turned to me and hands folded behind him. There is a huge World War I painting on the left-hand-side wall. This is the kind of art I expect Fielding to have. Grayson Fielding turns round. I am only just taller than him. He's got a pronounced belly that I missed from his internet images this morning. He's been developing that since his first business lunch in the City but the bags under his eyes might be new.

'Mr Mensah!' he says in a refined voice that is more high-pitched than it had been on the phone a couple of hours earlier. It is too hollow to be menacing.

'Thank you for coming,' Fielding says politely but as if he were my commanding officer in the army and goes to sit down behind his desk as he indicates I should do likewise. I sit down before he does.

Both his hands pinch the area of his trousers above his knees, holding the material as he bends to sit.

'Now let me get straight to the point.' He leans back in his chair. 'My wife is missing.'

Fielding hands me a file and staring out at me from page three is a passport photo of a Black woman so beautiful she would make a pastor kick a contribution box over.

Fielding continues, 'You have been recommended to me as a person who will be able to find her and will be discreet.'

I say nothing but glance back at the file he has given me. Women that look like her have problems God alone can solve.

I think about how I feel about my day and what I'm doing here. And I nod.

'My wife is originally from South Sudan and before I met

her mixed in very different circles in London to me, and it is in these circles, which I believe you are familiar with, where I think she will be found. I acquired a taste for the exotic and women from the lower classes, if I can put it that way, when I was in the Army. I know little of my wife's world, nor do I want to know, but I want her back.'

Alarm 2, a beautiful woman who the man can fall in love with brings him the work. Back to the file. In books the woman doesn't necessarily have to bring the case. It's enough that she's merely part of the story. Merely. I've never liked the word. I've never used it before but I want to give it a chance. It's as bad as I thought it was. There's nothing mere about this woman. I am definitely in trouble with this one. I know it.

It could be as I feared. This detective has a target he can't see on his chest.

Fielding looks at me trying to find a reaction as he continues, 'I would like you to find her for me please, as soon as possible.'

'Shit,' I think to myself.

Alarm 2

My head rings. Fielding's refined voice is too hollow to be shrill, but it doesn't make the ringing go away.

'Mr Mensah, I can find my wife without using your services, but I need all of this handled very carefully and with a delicacy that some of the resources I have at my disposal won't achieve in a search of this nature.'

He pauses. I watch him, very carefully.

'I have no idea where she is…'

I flick through the file mechanically while he talks as if to be polite, but I'm genuinely interested. She's only been in the UK for three years, but has already had a British passport for the last two. It's a very thorough file he has put together on his wife. The file lists where she has worked with addresses and contact names and gives details of small-scale business ventures. I visualise where I'll need stealth or muscle, and diligence if I'm pushed.

'I expect complete discretion on your part and total secrecy.'

I should ask him where he got my number from, or is that being indiscreet?

'Well,' I say, stroking my jaw. 'With every job like this there are some questions I could ask like how long has she been missing for, why do you think she's missing rather than left you, has she gone missing before, does she want to be found?'

I watch him in his seat, not reacting. His eyes are as hollow as his voice.

'But you wouldn't have come to me if you wanted to answer lots of questions.'

I lean back in my chair and watch to see how the man will react.

'The file should have all the details you'll need to know about her. Copies of her particulars and history I deemed relevant. Everything.'

'Everything?' I enquire.

'Everything that could possibly be pertinent. Her date of birth, National Insurance number, passport details and the like... everything you should need,' he repeats.

I get to the last page of Fielding's file and stop. Not just because there are no more pages, but the black and white photograph of a small house actually holds my attention. It's not a photocopy. It's an original black and white photograph. It's like the photos that used to be in the windows of estate agents. Her former work addresses might give me something, but I like this place for providing something... real. I can tell it's not in east or south London. North maybe, west probably.

Fielding observes the photograph I'm studying, and puts it in context.

'That is the house I established her in shortly after we had met and she became my mistress. When we got married I bought this present house for us. My wife liked the idea of living in The Bishop's Avenue. No doubt the house in the photograph will be of interest.'

He is still matter-of-fact but it does seem that he wants her back, for real. He hasn't said he loves her so I can't accuse him of lying about why he wants her back. He hasn't said he doesn't love her either. Men want to get wives, girlfriends and mistresses back all the time – for all types of reasons.

Looking at Fielding now, I try to find the danger I've spent the morning thinking he represents. I don't see it. He has a full head of silver-grey hair, but even with the bags under his eyes and his sagging belly he is quite handsome for an old rich white guy. He could be on the front of a hair-dye box if silver-grey hair ever becomes the in-thing.

'I met my wife just over two years ago when she was running away from the men that helped her come here who were pursuing her for money they claimed she still owed them. She would never tell me who they were. I told her I could deal with them, but she said it would be better for me if I didn't know.'

I listen to the second-hand tale of people-trafficking bogeymen with no names, and I like this woman from South Sudan straight away. This sounds like standard feed-the-white-man-type bullshit. It could easily be true, and if so then she is one of the women that figures out how powerless these gangs really are, and acts accordingly. She pulled a rich white man, refused to pay what she owed, and proceeded to live the high life. Also, if it is true, and men like that are involved, I will need a gun today.

I ask, 'Do you think she's still in danger from these men?'

'I honestly don't know. I offered to clear all her debts, but she knew they would keep coming back for more while there was more to get. I don't think she'd heard from them for a while. But it's there I think you should start your enquiries. These types of men... never write off their debts.'

I nod again.

'South Sudan eh...' I say it almost to myself trying to remember what little I knew of the place. 'These men. Were they Arabs or Black?' I hate tangling with Arabs. They can't wait to get to Allah, and the more warriors they can take with them the better.

'From what she said, Black... Black African,' Fielding replies.

Another reason he chose me. I'll get answers in places his people don't even know exist.

Unbidden, adrenaline starts to course through me. I don't try to stop it but instead control it and let it get to my fingertips so that I'm fully ready for whatever Fielding is bringing me into. It's going to be a lively day. The feeling of doom that's been disturbing me all morning is still there, but I know – no, I feel – that I'm going to give the demon the worthiest run for its money.

I think Fielding is being straight with me, as straight as a man like him can be. But still, there is no way Fielding's call today was as simple as he's trying to make it seem. 'I am fairly certain that they or certainly their affiliates... have her. If that is the case, I want you to rescue her, and as quietly as possible. And make certain that those who have her don't present a problem in the future. Is that clear?'

'It's clear,' I tell Fielding. 'Ensuring that certain problems are not present in the future will be expensive though.'

'I will pay you two hundred thousand pounds for this undertaking. And an extra fifty thousand if you return her to me within forty-eight hours. That should cover any extra considerations?'

Two hundred and fifty thousand. That's Alarm 3.

Extra considerations. He means if I have to kill a lot of men.

I realise that Alarm 1 is not an alarm any more. This job doesn't seem at all easy, and the client here needs me.Why send someone else when he can send me?

'Mr Mensah?' Fielding asks, 'Can you help me?'

'I can.' I don't like promising to deliver. I almost always do but I feel taking the client's money is enough of a promise on my part.

A quarter of a million is more money than I have ever been paid for any one job. If I open my mouth and pretend to haggle, I'll give it away. Better to remain silent and have Fielding suspect this than open my mouth and remove all doubt.

I shut the file and reply, 'You'll hear from me as soon as I've got something to tell you. That will be soon.' I turn back to a subject I don't mind him knowing I take seriously, 'How much of a retainer do I get up front?'

'I was thinking twenty-five,' he says matter-of-factly, obviously not embarrassed to discuss payment terms.

'I was thinking one hundred and twenty-five.'

'That's half,' he points out.

I think about it for a second, looking around the room. 'Yes. Yes it is half.'

'Why, for someone who makes the money you do, you might be tempted to take the money and run.'

'Why would I not finish the job when I've got more of the same waiting for me in the safe behind the portrait somewhere?'

Fielding pauses then asks, 'Will you accept a cheque for a hundred?'

'I'm not sure if my bank accepts cheques any more.'

'I'll get you cash.'

'That'll probably be best.'

He leaves the room to get my money. My attention pans back to the big World War I painting. Its title card reads: '*Gassed* by John Singer Sargeant'. Dozens of British soldiers in it are standing and holding crutches, and some are lying on the ground, arms in slings. All of them have bandaging around their heads and eyes. The blind leading the blind.

The only man in the painting not injured is wearing a non-military tunic. The man, probably a medic, is directing the walking wounded to safety. In road slang gas means to lie or exaggerate and gassed means to be lied to. A wicked thought occurs to me, that maybe the healthy looking medic is counting and misdirecting the now useless soldiers, before he abandons them and runs back to wherever he was when they were attacked in the first place.

Is Fielding the medic? I know he's lying to me, but I don't know about what.

Fielding returns with more than a hundred thousand pounds in a pouch the size of a boot bag which I take from him. I don't insult either of us by counting it. I walk out of the room wondering if I should stow the cash first or start on the search.

The woman he wants me to find is named Buki Nneka.

Somebody bring me back some guns please

I'm so in awe of how little I've got my head around my morning that I have no real memory of how I got from the north

London suburbs to where I am now, back in familiar Hackney territory. I negotiate side streets named after old English earls at a time when the African reverse colonisation of low-rise estates along Sandringham and Amhurst wasn't anticipated. I welcome the distraction when an object that might be closer than it appears makes itself known in my left-wing mirror.

A red motorbike.

A red motorbike comes alongside matching my speed, then effortlessly floats in front of me. Without looking back the motorbike rider pulls up in front of my car, and stops quickly in a burning mix of hot rubber, tarmac and engine oils.

I hit the brakes hard enough to bare my teeth. When I'm sure that I won't hit him and the car behind me won't hit me, the rider is off his red motorbike and crouched in front of my car. I look at my rear-view mirror and I look back through the windscreen in front of me. The rider sticks one finger up at me and converts it to two-fingered gunny fingers. And then my car is moved, upward, and I realise it is being towed with me in it. My first thought is that I've never been in a car being towed before.

The who and why don't matter. I grip the sides of my seat. Then I try to take my seatbelt off before looking to open the door, when we turn fast once, twice more, and I'm gripping the sides of my seat again.

I'm getting my heart rate down to something practical, and my left thumb has released the seatbelt when my car stops, and all my work trying to free myself only benefits what looks like a young man with a scarf over the lower half of his face, as he drags me out of the car. How I'm going to fight stops being a question when another bad guy dressed like the first helps him, and they push me against a cold brick wall. My right arm is forced up against my spine.

'Where are the God damn guns?' a man who's neither of them asks.

I can't see the speaker's face, but I can see in my peripheral vision he's built like a big loudspeaker in a club: large, rectangular and black in expensive fitted wool and platinum.

'What?' I ask as I feel my arm bent even harder behind me. I grimace but try not to make a fuss.

'Our guns. Where are they?' he repeats slowly.

I recognise him now.

It's Mossi. I don't know if it's his real name and if so whether it's his first or last. The same name thing goes with the man he works for – Cromber, but I know who they are. They are the biggest crew of drug dealers in east London right now. The realisation makes me wonder if the commandeering of my car had happened too quickly for somebody to call the police. I've never requested the police for my own salvation but them coming here with sirens blaring would be a welcome distraction.

'Your boy Klu's back on the road but all this time my boy Tony's nowhere to be seen.'

I nod and ask, 'Is it true?'

'What?' Mossi asks.

'Word on the streets is Tony confessed to some war crimes type stuff and was chased off by serious police, Scotland Yard and ting.'

'Heh.' Mossi says looking at me hard. 'That's what the streets are saying!'

I continue to nod, only slower, 'On account of him killing a bunch of people and raping women in some war they had back in… where was he from again?… Malawi, right?'

Mossi says nothing.

'It's good that he went into hiding then,' I muse. 'Instead

of using info on you and Cromber here as leverage with the police. He didn't take you lot down too, he must have been a good man after all!'

'I've been speaking to him,' Mossi says then stops as if for a reaction.

'In Malawi?' I ask.

'On the phone, Tony said it was you. He told me, it was you that sent him back to Malawi. He told me you put one gun to his face and another gun to his dick, and made him record that confession admitting to the video camera all that shit he was wanted for down there, then made him sign the envelope you posted to the police.' Mossi doesn't let me say anything before shouting, 'Then he told me that you put him in that shipping container we had coming here.'

'It wasn't me,' I deny it all of course.

'Nate, what did you do with the guns?'

'It wasn't me.'

'All those guns! Guns that fire bullets like these…' Mossi holds thumb and forefinger apart wavering between three to five inches. 'Fuckin' armour piercing calibre… go through more niggas than Angelina before they get tired!'

During my conversation with Mossi my eyes have been scanning the space under the railway arch. The scaffolding, poles and an interesting business logo I want to take more notice of but can't because I know exactly how the next ten seconds are going to go.

Next, I wonder where exactly the motorbike goon who did the job with my car is. His location and job are important because I'm about to deal with this second goon whose job it is to hold me while Mossi lectures. A lot of people don't know the reasons why police hold and cuff you tight. It's so that the pain doesn't allow room for the thought of escape in your head. This guy's hold on me weakens with every second of Mossi's speech. And handcuffs don't get bored.

Picking my time and place, I punch him very hard in the throat. Shocked, his hands travel up to his neck, but I interrupt... Elbow first, I shove him backwards so that I can kick him in the nose.

Mossi is on me now, I duck and have space behind me, but I don't use the advantage right away. Mossi is very big, but it's muscle, that means he's not as agile as me.

Mossi will expect me to attack him, because running isn't our style in this business, but I run away to appeal to his ego. I run under partially erected scaffolding with Mossi right behind me. Thinking quickly, I try to give Mossi the impression that I want to grab hold of one of the scaffolding bars to lever myself out of this metal jungle. That's actually plan B.

But plan A is to get a piece of the scaffolding as a weapon. But the piece I selected doesn't give. It had looked loose but it's actually an effective piece of scaffolding, and useless to me. The next piece of scaffolding jutting out from a stack of a dozen others comes loose in my hands even more easily than I'd hoped it would.

The scaffolding is light, or I've underestimated my strength and how pissed off I am, and I connect with Mossi's elbow. We both hear, for me, a highly satisfying crunch. Mossi howls, curses and swears oaths under his breath. I take a look up to see if motorbike boy comes running but he doesn't. Mossi starts to move so I swing again at my original target – Mossi's knee. People never chase you with a busted knee, but they do with a hurt arm. Not something you learn from watching action films. Again I miss, this time hitting Mossi's thigh. Mossi looks back up at me with none of the menace of seven seconds ago. He looks down at his arm, maybe his thigh, then back at me and back to his arm again. Mossi wants to ignore the pain, but a second later he looks down and we both see his misaligned lower arm. It's broken.

'You appear to be experiencing some difficulties,' I say. 'Leave me and Klu alone, and we'll say no more about this, shall we?' I nod and slowly back away from him and the systematic grunts he's producing.

My car is still hooked up to the tow truck, but the two vehicles are close and all four wheels of my somehow unscathed car sit on the ground. I unhook the slack tow cable and I check my face in the wing mirror. I can feel a cut on the inside of my lip, but that won't show, and there are no cuts or bruises.

The yellow scarf around goon two's face is spattered with blood, but I take it anyway, and wipe my hands and polish off the other smudges on my car.

Absurdly, I see I've left dirty fingerprints on his ski jacket. I throw him the used scarf and I sincerely hope this boy doesn't get himself killed until he's washed this a few times.

As I reverse away from the innocuous but powerful truck, I reflect on the ingenious plan of forcibly towing a car. You could waylay somebody you wanted to talk to who didn't want to talk to you in broad daylight, and nobody, apart from maybe the following car, would look twice. And possibly an observant CCTV monitor. I hear a siren somewhere in the cool London air and accelerate away hard. I don't want to explain to the police what has happened here any more than Mossi and company will want to. What nearly happened could have been a professionally painful ordeal, if these guys knew what they were doing.

As I wonder whether to tell Klu about this I look again at that interesting business logo. It appears to be a hand cupped around a house and it's everywhere on the site. The rider of the red motorbike, still wearing his helmet with the reflective visor darts, is now a lookout with his back mostly to me and the ambush site. I see his astonishment, not through the reflective visor but in the flustered way his neck jerks the helmet. I return his previous one digit salute with a good natured thumbs-up, but really I'm wondering what to do about Klu.

I hadn't thought Tony would stay alive for long enough to make a full report back to London but now it all comes back to bite me today.

I feel that by not telling Klu that Cromber and Mossi are looking for us after all, he can't get ready for what's coming. But Klu was always ready, and telling him means he would definitely go after them when I know, given time, I can think of a smart way out of it. If there is a smart way of dealing with east London's newest and most savage crew of drug dealers. Drug dealers who are very annoyed that I took their guns. I flex the arm I had folded behind my back and use it to work a phone.

CALLING... DEDEI

Dedei. The woman who launched a hundred beefs. Klu versus Tony. Me versus Tony. And now me versus Mossi.

'Hello.' Dedei sounds like she's sulking. She's a Spike Lee version of Princess Peach, unaware of all the mayhem she incites for the Super Mario brothers with the Bowsers of this world. And there's nothing Nintendo about this game we're about to play.

'Tell your mum I'm sorry I've missed her calls,' I say.

''kay.'

'...And tell her...' I try not to pause too long, 'to keep Klu close today.'

''kay,' she replies taking more interest in the conversation than she's shown so far.

'Cool. Later, then.'

Dedei hangs up.

Later.

I'm not so much assuming that Cromber or Mossi won't make a move on Klu if he's at his mum's, but there'd be a direct line to me if they did.

I wonder why Cromber's people haven't made their move before.

Cromber only appeared on the scene a year or so ago. Not long enough to have loyal people behind bars, and so maybe they were waiting for Klu to come out.

This was their move, now. They would have been better off not making it at all.

I estimate I have until about 5.00 pm to decide what's to be done about Mossi and them. 5.00 pm is when gangsters get ready for work.

Cherchez la femme

There are three numbers from Grayson Fielding's file that belonged to Buki Nneka's phones. Up to three phones, switched off… I, in theory wouldn't of course have been needed if she was answering her phone and promising to be back soon. I've chosen to kick things off by visiting a community business centre, made up of small social enterprises and charities in Stratford. Buki Nneka used to lease a unit here in her humbler days.

The community business centre I am in front of now holds the last of the borough's creative hustlers amongst the wine bars of Newham. Somewhere in the building is the sound of children learning to make sorrel juice. There are a handful of people sitting inside in their cubicles eating homemade croissants. I am generally ignored as I go in search of unit 8.

At the door to unit 8 there is a gap around the replaced lock. I nudge the door with my shoulder and there's some give. The door has seen better days. A half-hearted kick would be enough to break it in, again.

'Finally! It's about time you came!' A woman's voice, 'It's been almost a month since we called you!'

Keeping my hands in my pockets, I turn slowly, so that the speaker will not think she has made a mistake. Her belief that I am from the police should work in my favour.

I respond with an enigmatic, 'Hmm...?'

The woman's face holds an expression that matches the tone she speaks with. Hard and cold. She isn't at all what anybody would call pretty, but judging from her build and legs she probably jogs for half an hour every day.

'I go where I'm sent, ma'am!'

'We get broken into and you do nothing! Hooligans came through here and spray-painted all-sorts of filth all over the building, and you police just don't care!'

'Please accept my apologies for the delay. You have my attention now.'

Impersonating a Police Officer
Maximum Penalty: 6 months imprisonment and/or fine
Police Act 1996, Section 90

She tries to direct me to the scene of the recent vandalism.

'Did anybody get a look at the yobs?'

'Yes! I said so on the phone. About four kids – couldn't have been older than thirteen, any of them. I chased them. They got away on bikes.'

I keep incredulity at the vagueness of the description off

my face by thinking about yobs breaking into the car outside of the apartment block where I live this morning.

'I think I know them. There have been other similar complaints. We'll get them, but first I'm going to have to start investigating here. Unit 8,' I insist.

The woman grimaces, 'It's empty now and it got broken into weeks ago. That hardly matters any more as the tenant is long gone.'

'All the same, I'm going to have to ask you to open this door.'

Slowly and grudgingly, she produces a bunch of keys big enough to have a key for every unit in here.

The door opens and I'm hit by the smell of damp walls and ageing cloth.

I'm impressed by the amount of materials left behind by Ms Nneka and the burglar. Obviously Ms Nneka didn't have to care after she got her millionaire Fielding. My concern is that some jammy burglar has stolen something that could lead me to Buki Nneka's current whereabouts. I sigh an unhappy sigh as I foresee having to menace some idiot who may have sold on anything useful already.

The tricky burglaries are the ones when things that are clearly of some resale value are not taken but left. This is one of them. Granted, most of what is left would need transit vans or larger vehicles to transport away. The long poles of silk would be of value to somebody, as would the other white elephants in here. It could have been anybody, a lot of anybodies if there was more than one break-in. All of them without big get-away vehicles.

One thing is for sure, I want to find whoever broke in here because the whens, whys and what-did-they-take might be very useful in finding Buki. I don't know this for a fact, but it might be as useful a starting point as the others I've got lined up for today.

'Just because our community business centre follows a non-standard and socially-aware business model, you think we don't count!' She speaks more slowly than most Londoners, even though she's angry. Londoners like to talk really fast. Too slow and somebody else has said what they want to say. Talk fast and hopefully nobody actually catches how full of shit they are.

'They don't go and rob the Tesco next door, but if they had, I bet you'd have been over there like a shot!'

I hope this woman isn't going to make me regret being mistaken for a police officer. I like getting access to places and getting people to answer questions they think the law says they have to.

'Did the last tenant keep valuable equipment here?'

'I don't think so!' She sneers, 'All this was just for appearances for her type of people. They're not really involved with our movement.'

'Her type of people...' I nod. And for the first time I take my hands out of my pockets. The woman grudgingly admires the white surgical gloves I sport, and the Ziploc bags and fingerprint dust and brush I take from my bag. On my knees, on my toes and bent over I dust areas with high potentiality for prints of value. I even dust the headless mannequin, mostly for a laugh but maybe it was a pervert that was here.

Perverts are notoriously easy to bully. When I stick a piece of tape to an area that produces a partial or full print I place it in one of the Ziploc bags and scribble on the side of the bag what surface I've taken it off. I do that for the benefit of the eagle-eyed woman.

Within ten minutes I've identified about a dozen sets of

usable fingerprints and two times as many partials – finger and thumb tips and sides. There is no point checking for prints on the doors as the woman explains they had to change the locks.

'Her and her squat in Hackney!'

'I beg your pardon?'

'The last tenant, Ms Nneka. She told everybody she used to live in a squat in Hackney!' The woman assumes correctly that I haven't been paying attention before now, 'But it turned out all along she was granted full citizenship when she arrived so the council had given her a place of her own, in one of those part-mortgage-part-rent properties out there. She illegally sublet it and used the proceeds to live with her friends in Chelsea.' She pronounces Chelsea as if it is almost as dirty a word as Hackney.

'Really?'

Who would claim to be from Hackney who wasn't?

'Where have you been forwarding her post?'

'Post! She only sold a few dresses. The closest she got to repeat business was that character from the music studio.'

'Studio?'

'Hmm! Fitz Beatz Studio. I can't remember his name... he was here often enough. Said he owned a studio in Shoreditch but I wasn't sure he was interested in her singing at first.'

There wasn't any music studio or an address in Shoreditch in Fielding's file.

'What did this guy look like?'

'Oh you know the type! Hair gel, tight suit, shirt open for his chest hair to breathe.'

'When did you last see her... and where?'

'Where?' the woman asked her eyes deepening in suspicion.

'Here,' I say, 'or anywhere...'

'Can I see your ID again?' she asks.

She hadn't seen my ID. It is obviously time I should be leaving.

'That won't be necessary. When the uniforms arrive tell them DCI Roacher has already printed this room.'

'Your name's Roacher?' she relaxes a little.

I smiled in reply and added, 'You should tell CSI to focus their dusting on the vandalised units especially... which unit are you?'

'Unit 13.'

'Paying special attention to unit 13.'

She looks appeased.

I'm leaving with a bagful of usable prints, including Buki's no doubt. Realistically no professional would leave behind their prints but I've done a good job of trying to put myself in the position of idiot thieves and where they'd place their unprotected hands. I look forward to meeting them as much as I look forward to getting away from this woman who seems determined to escort me to the exit. Then again maybe I've been dealing with high calibre operators capable of making Buki disappear, safe in the knowledge that they couldn't be traced. I want to meet them too.

I turn to the woman as I leave her building and her company, 'You don't happen to have CCTV here, do you?'

The Searcher

As I manoeuvre through east London I look at everybody and everything that my quest takes me past. Buki Nneka is not going to be the easiest person to find but find her I will. London is like a stush woman. It's a city that isn't inclined to help you until it's sure it's going to be worth its while. But say the right thing at the right time in the right place and you could get a result beyond your wildest expectations.

I've just finished visiting Ms Nneka's former employers. Before the quantum leap that was marriage to Fielding, Buki had been improving her station in life all by herself, one retail job at a time. Her jobs improved over two years – no doubt matching her improving English and a need for access to a nicer line in clothes.

She had started with cash-in-hand work in Redbridge, the eastern-most point in Buki Nneka's travels in London. The French lady in charge said Buki hadn't had much to talk to her about. I got even less from the boutique in a shopping street near Mile End. Buki's last job before venturing out to make her own clothes was a store that was part of a chain. That was in The Eastfield, an upmarket Olympics-is-coming sized mall that would never usually be seen outside west London or a suburb with low overheads. Buki's colleagues were mostly students trying to supplement their student loans, while Buki had gotten herself fixed up with a rich man in the City, adroitly adapting to the life of a mistress before becoming his wife.

All the people Buki had worked with agreed on only two things about her. One, Buki hadn't talked about her past that much and what she did say revealed little. Two, a lot of men had come looking for Buki in the days after she left.

I make no assumptions as to why, because they might stop me from looking for those little things about her that could put me ahead of others in the race.

Her third and final job was at a branch in Canary Wharf. Buki worked there as a sales assistant. I think about going to Canary Wharf but decide to leave it until later if it's still necessary. Maybe my visit to the Eastfield branch is being discussed and reported right now preparing them for any potential visit I might make to Canary Wharf. There's another reason I don't go to Canary Wharf and it's the grey three-door

Korean car following me.

Except for the tints it's like every other car on the road. It annoys me that I may have subconsciously dismissed it because it's a non-police, non-gangster car. As a result I can't now be sure how long it's been following me. I hadn't seen it parked at the Stratford community business centre. But I wouldn't have done if it had arrived after I did.

I intentionally don't let my eye rest on it for long.

I can always tell when somebody I'm following has figured out they're being followed. The body language between someone who suspects they're being followed and someone who knows they're being followed is completely different and if the person in that grey car knows the difference I don't want them realising I know, until I'm ready. I tell myself I've been nowhere really important, but I can't be sure.

I don't think my questions would have provoked much interest but I hate mistakes. The driver could have gone in after me, everywhere I've been, to ask about me and what I wanted. He probably knows I'm looking for a Buki Nneka and unless he's good, which I know he isn't from the sloppy way he is following me, he will raise suspicions.

My blue Audi is very nice but I have to be honest and admit that a lot of cars look like it. Because of that, I get a couple of seconds grace after using the most evasive manoeuvres until they see the wrong number plate or a bald Asian man in a turtleneck.

Then two calls vie for my attention.

MERLEY CALLING...

That call I will ignore as a matter of course.

UNKNOWN NUMBER CALLING...

I haven't saved Fielding's number but it's not that particular unknown number. It may be the driver I've just lost calling me to ask where I've got to.

'Yeah,' I answer.

'Is this Mr Nathan Mensah?' an out-of-breath voice enquires. I can tell because it's quiet beyond the sound of his breathing that the owner of the voice is most certainly not behind the wheel of a car, Korean or otherwise.

'Who's calling?' I ask.

'Er, you don't know me but you've been recommended to me. I need help – I'm about to get arrested.'

I relax a little, 'This is your phone call and you're calling me?'

'I was driving and they tried to pull me over. I had five kilo...'

'I haven't heard that and you haven't said it,' I interrupt.

'I parked the car before they could look in the boot. I work for...'

'No names,' I say, pissed off he's already put mine out there. 'Where are you?'

'In some chick's place in Wanstead Flats. One time chased me from Romford Road.'

'Blimey! You must be tired!'

'I go to the gym!' He sounds better, now I know his personal habits he feels we've gotten to know each other so he can speak freely, 'They've surrounded the block. I can't get out.'

Even though I won't get paid for this one I feel compelled to help a brother in need. I am most impressed that he has had my number or one of the numbers that redirects to this one and he hasn't called me before to make gangster small-talk. I can't say too much without running the risk of being seen as an accessory if this is a recorded set-up.

'Here's the thing. Car or no car, what they've got they've got. If they've got enough to send you to jail – then you're going to jail. Do you understand what I'm saying to you?'

'I-I-I think so.'

I can hear him regretting every blasé prison joke he's ever made.

I continue the briefing, 'If they take you to Stoke Newington Police Station – then they're coming at you straight. If they take you to Clapton then they'll be trying to get you to admit to something you haven't done or to tell stories about your friends. Do you understand what I'm saying to you?'

He doesn't understand what I'm saying to him because he then makes a sound that's a whisper or a groan, 'They would've found the…'

'It can go down as an illegal search,' I point out realistically.

'Illegal? But it's the police, bluhd?'

'They make illegal searches all the time. What car is it, a Benz?'

'Lexus.'

'Black right?' I can cut through all the politically correct bullshit.

'Ya, dunno!'

'Tints on four?'

'Standard.'

'What's wrong with it?' I ask.

'Not a fuckin' thing fam. Rolled off a showroom in Knightsbridge last week fam!'

I now know that matey was pulled over by the police for any number of reasons that don't necessarily mean they know he has what he wants to say he does not have in the boot. There's every chance they hadn't noticed he was Black in a tinted gangster's choice of car until he took off. I've known cases like this where a young brother like this says nothing to the police and thirty-six hours later goes and finds his car right where he's left it, half on a pavement somewhere, and still with nothing wrong with it that the police can use as probable cause for a vehicle stop and search.

'Now, do you drink tea or coffee or anything like that?'

'Er, no, not really. Why? Should I?'

'No,' I command, 'When the police take you, don't take a cup or can or bottle or anything they offer you to drink. They will want your fingerprints and if they can't ink you legit they'll lift them off your beverage of choice. That's a free drink that will cost you if they're desperate enough. 'Don't touch anything they give you. Don't even shake the plainclothesman's hand when they walk in to question you.'

I can't tell if he's nodding but the young brother's breathing seems to be under control and there seem to be no pressing questions. Those are good signs that he understands what I'm telling him.

All the same, I review, 'What are you going to tell the police?'

'Nothing!' he answers.

It is all very well remaining silent but if no-name on the other end of the line has no real reason to remain silent the reasons the police will soon present for not remaining silent will all become more reasonable.

'Why d'you not talk to the police?'

'It's the p'lice innit!'

'But why d'you not talk to the 'p'lice'?'

'P'lice don't care.'

'No.' He's right but it's not the answer I'm looking for.

'P'lice are liars!'

'No.' He's right again but still not the answer I'm looking for.

'P'lice are racist!'

'No.' I hope this litany of actually right but wrong answers will not go on for long. We presumably do not have long before the thin blue line he has outrun snaps into place around him. It is essential my man on the other end of this line produces the answer himself. I am just another voice that will talk at him today.

'Bruv, p'lice just want to lock me up.' He sounds as exasperated with me as with his situation.

That is close enough.

That's the problem with playing guessing games. The most obvious reason isn't put out there because of its obviousness.

I follow his point through, 'There's nothing just about it. They don't give a fuck about what you've done and they don't give a fuck about you. They want to send you to jail for the longest time possible or they want you to work for them or both. They're going to do whatever it takes. Beat you up if they can get away with it, pretend to be your friend, tell you whatever it takes to have you where they want you today.'

It's with consternation that I realise that the grey Korean three-door has found me again. I have a newly acquired respect for the driver, despite his inability to keep himself hidden from me.

'Here's the thing man,' I end by repeating the counsel from somewhere near the beginning of our talk, 'Maybe they know nothing and maybe they have it all but nothing you say will get you out from under.' I get creative driving around the Bromley by Bow interchange, 'So that's why you say nothing to the police.'

He responds in an all-conversation high tone, 'You right! You right! I'm a no-comment for these wanker muthafuckaz!'

'Probably best to just say nothing,' I reply adding my finishing touch and speeding away from what I'm hoping is a now lost-again driver of the grey car 'Take it easy with those no comments. It makes cops think you think you're smarter than them and that there's something to comment on. Handle them carefully. Don't make them think too hard.'

'They're coming,' he whispers and the line goes dead before I can wish him good luck.

I check to make sure I'm not being followed by the Korean and pay more than usual attention to my rear-view mirror as I go in search of the man with a studio that the woman at the community business centre spoke of.

Undercover Brother

I park as close to the Fitz Beatz Studio in Shoreditch as I can.

An eleven or twelve-year-old sits on her stationary bike feeding herself plantain crisps. She admires my car and scrutinises me as I step out of it.

'How much to make sure nobody fucks widdit?' I say gesturing at my car and the council estates nearby.

'Fifteee pounds,' she says shaking her bag of crisps and peering at the bottom.

'That's a lot!' I say, genuinely surprised at her asking price.

'That car's a lot too innit!'

I shake my head at her mercenary attitude and take my money clip out of my pocket. Her smile disappears as I peel off a twenty pound note, holding it out to her and return the rest of my money to my pocket.

'That's a twenty!'

I nod. 'Yeah, buy a ticket for twenty minutes or thirty – whatever the machines do out here and keep the change.'

'I said fifteen!' she says still examining the transparent bag showing us both it's empty.

'Oh, I thought you said fifteen!'

'Nah I said fifteee!'

'I thought you said fifteen.' I insist still holding out the same twenty. She flinches first and swearing under her breath she snatches the note from me.

'Why aren't you at school anyway?'

'School's off,' she replies spraying crumbs over her acquired note.

I nod.

It's a ten minute walk to Fitz Beatz Studio. Lining the studio walls are pictures of all the somebodies who other somebodies had told they can sing. The out-of-shape white boy at reception watches me approach in the way receptionists size up customers in the hope their workload isn't about to be added to too much.

He has Shoreditch-type earrings that have made huge holes in his ear lobes, an inch in diameter. He speaks with the strongest cockney accent I've heard in years, the kind not heard around Shoreditch since the seventies.

'I want to talk to your boss.'

'Mr Fitz?' He looks me up and down. 'Who may I ask is calling?'

'My name's Nathan Mensah. Do you know who Customs & Excise are?'

His eyes round out and he swallows.

Earrings picks up the phone and tells the man on the other end, 'There's a man here. He says he's from Customs & Excise.'

I nod to myself.

Earrings comes off the phone and points to his left and gives me directions.

'Cheers,' I say and I stroll past walls with a lot of awards

I've never heard of.

The door with a granite-finish sign reads: *Patrick Fitz –
General Manager.* The door is already wide open so I walk
into the office without knocking.

Not quite hiding behind the door is a man who spends
enough time in the gym so that his five-foot-eight frame
doesn't seem as short as all that. He is wearing a blue two-tone
brocade material suit and purple shirt.

'Hello there!' he says taking my hand and pumping it
effusively.

I get ready. I predict everything he is going to tell me is
going to be a lie and if not a direct lie, not the truth, more
commonly known as bullshit.

'This is a nice studio you've set up, Mr Fitz.' I sit on
his chair and admire the password prompt on his computer
flatscreen.

'Call me Patrick.' He doesn't like the idea of sitting in one
of his guest seats so remains standing for the time being. 'Can
I get you something to drink? Tea? Coffee?'

'Pineapple juice,' I say, looking around.

'I understand you're from C and E.' Fitz says with over-
practised ease.

I don't deny this.

Impersonating a Customs and Excise Officer
Maximum Penalty: 2 years imprisonment and a fine
Customs and Excise Management Act 1979 section 13

Legitimate businesses fear Customs and Excise even more
than dodgy businesses. The police can only take your life or
your liberty. Nobody quite knows what a Customs and Excise
Officer is allowed to do but they know that hypothetically, he

cannot only arrest people but also do some really awkward things like request receipts and all documentation since commencement of trading.

'What can I do for you?' His smile is too wide for a man not refusing me a loan or wanting my vote. 'I can assure you all my VAT returns are in order.'

He runs a hand through his hair. That's the third time he's done this in the minute since I've been in the room. It gives him a different look after each pass. He hands me a glass of pineapple juice which I'm not sure will be safe to drink.

'I'm enquiring into your dealings and tax arrangements with Ms Buki Nneka.'

'Oh! Buki!' He is surprised and relieved at the limited scope of my business. He pauses for a moment, 'Oh it's her you're investigating is it? I can't say I'm not relieved. Nobody likes being audited. She used to drop by all the time, she fancied herself as a singer. Eventually… it made sense to give her a deal, but we hadn't got to the stage where someone at my level would work with her.'

'I see,' I say, but I don't. 'So those rumours that you were… good friends…' I swill the pineapple around my glass, 'those would be unfounded would they? Good friends have been known to do favours for each other in the area of hiding money, assets and keeping secrets and the like…'

'Oh, no no no! You couldn't be more wrong, believe me.'

I don't.

'Ours was a strictly business relationship. Any trouble she's gotten herself into is nothing to do with us… I mean me and her… we were never…'

From Fitz's spinning seat I again take in the full view of the office as well as the small garden of miniature Japanese trees. Inspection finished I focus on Fitz and I quote him, 'Any trouble she might have gotten herself into... What kind of trouble are you thinking Ms Nneka's in?'

Fitz eases his shoulders into a slight shrug. 'I'm sure I don't know.'

'I believe Mr Grayson Fielding is the proprietor of Fitz Beatz Studios?'

I mention the older richer man whose Sudanese wife this joker may have been sharing. Fitz looks at me hard, neglecting to run his hand through his hair.

'No, Mr Fielding has no interest in the studios. I am the sole proprietor.'

I hope I don't let on that I'm throwing him questions randomly. The hand through the hair thing might be a tell-tale sign of impatience and discomfort or it might point to dishonesty. He's not a very good liar and it's obvious he's not telling the truth, but about what, I have no way of knowing. Everybody hides something – especially from the government.

'What did you say your name was?' Fitz asks as he hands me a card with his accountant's name written on it.

'Nathan Mensah. I may be back,' I tell him as I leave, thinking of the best way to break in.

Before that I contemplate bribing his assistant Earrings on the off chance there's some useful gossip. What was Buki Nneka's role here, and could it have contributed in any way to her disappearing?

I don't shake off the odd sense of sleaze I feel until after I leave the office, then the building and see a parked black cab and black Range Rover facing away from each other in a three-car bay under the Old Street railway bridge. I step between the two vehicles and unhook the buttons of my trousers. The Shoreditch citizenry walk past in a way they walk past men urinating in public. They pointedly stare away and go about their business. There are no grumbles about my lack of manners or the direction the world is going in. I pretend to do up my trouser buttons, certain that nobody will be able to describe me to the police when the owners of the Range Rover possibly realise I've cloned their number plates.

Back at my car, the young girl on leave from school has forgiven my bad hearing.

'Are the police looking for you?' she says between munches of a new bag of plantain crisps.

'I don't know, are they?'

'There was some dude drove past here three or four or maybe even five times.' She adds looking into her bag, 'I think it was a dude – I couldn't really see but the way he was driving slow when he passed this,' she points at my car, 'it's like he was looking for you.'

'And you think it was a police dude?' I press the remote for the car.

'Nah,' she thinks about it, 'the police don't use any shit China cars do they? I'm just saying…'

'Was it grey, the car?' I ask as she begins to pedal away, already knowing the answer.

She nods and pulls up her handlebars so that the bicycle balances on it's back wheel, and she exits my story on one wheel.

Dactylograph Park

I head for Lauriston. Lauriston isn't the smartest man I know but he has the ability to recall information like nobody else I've ever met. Lauriston's will be the first really friendly face I've seen today. Especially if I exclude my bruv Klu. Lauriston is always in southernmost Hackney between Victoria Park and Broadway Market.

From inside a gastro-food café bar I look around at the half-dozen men with the same fashionably faded T-shirts, Boho haircuts and half-chewed fruit logos on their devices as Lauriston. But he isn't to be seen here. It's approaching twelve o'clock and I speculate where he is to be found. The backstairs take me past the toilets on the first floor to the gym on the second.

Lauriston is alone in the middle of the room in a painful-looking yoga position.

'Nate fuckin' Mensah!' Lauriston breathes.

I hope the thing he's doing with one thigh and the other knee will spare him trying to take my hand and do all kinds of finger folding like he has seen African Americans do in movies. I'm wrong.

'I like the new sled!' he inclines his head towards the cars passing two storeys below. All the walls of the gym have ground-to-ceiling glass and through two of the windows he can see over to the park on the other side of the road.

'Wassup?' I ask.

'The sky, pimps and petrol prices! Those are up. The ground, hoes and quality of life are down.' Lauriston changes his pose before continuing, 'Have you been out for a drive in Hackney's wide, green and open spaces this morning?'

'Something like that,' I reply.

'You should enjoy all of it while you can. Word is some big development company's going to come and take all the little parks and open spaces in the borough for housing. New properties for people like me.'

I raise my eyebrow at him silently. Too many of my days are like this… Klu trying to make a real local criminal out of me and Lauriston, with his hacking, trying to plant and fertilise an upwardly-mobile social conscience like his inside me.

'I have always liked you! Even though when we were at university you knocked me out that time.'

'I thought we agreed you would stop going on about that. There's a limit to how many times I can say I'm sorry.'

Lauriston moves into another yoga pose.

'Me and you were the same back then! Outcasts, misfits. Your parents had given you up for adoption, and my parents had given up on me. I had the goth thing going on. You had the fake FUBU Hilfiger thing, but now you walk amongst them. You look like them, they give you their women.' Lauriston runs out of steam, as he settles into his pose. 'You fit in now! How did you do it?'

'I don't think I do fit in.'

'If you and I were to meet now we would never be friends.'

I disagreed. 'We would if I knew you were one of the best hackers going.'

'Anyway what can I do you for?'

I produce a brown envelope and leave it next to him. Lauriston takes it with relish, opens it and peers at the cellophane swatches inside them.

'These are fingerprints I lifted this morning.'

Lauriston peers at the cellophane samples like the girl on the bike had looked at her plantain crisps. 'Where did you get these from?'

'My bag,' I answer simply.

'I don't want to know, eh?' Lauriston asks bouncing his eyebrows happily.

'Probably, you do,' I shrug. 'The prints… I need word in two hours.'

'It will take at least ninety minutes!' Lauriston smiles at me, 'The usual rate?'

I nod, 'Bill me.'

He puts his hand out to shake mine, but I don't shake hands with men with their buttocks and one leg in the air so Lauriston points at me with the index fingers of both hands, his thumbs jerking like revolver hammers. It's an improbable yoga pose.

Maybe I need a change of attitude and investigative style, perhaps even a different jacket and a new car.

KLU CALLING...

Klu starts after I hit the green button but before I'm able to put the handset to my ear.

'When are you coming to see mum?' Mindful of what I told him earlier Klu adds quickly, 'And it has to be today!'

I ignore him as I change the subject. 'What's the word on the street?' I am very curious to find out how gangsters on their day to day are being affected by the two dead women.

'Nothing much couz... but there is some crazy talk that both chicks got done by some new shottas for hire. You heard of The Shampoo Crew?'

'The Shampoo Crew?' I try to stop from snorting. This already sounds like one of those conspiracies Klu is so fond of.

'Yeah, The Shampoo Crew! Like proper bona fide hit men.' When I don't say anything, Klu continues. 'This crew left guns behind at the scene and all sorts but that don't help 'cau' they were both clean apart from the chicks they just killed. Bruv, clean guns? In our blocks? And ain't no tourists get shot down here. That's some probably MI5 shit there or probably CIA! Deep!'

It was always going to be deep when the women are not from around this way. Klu was right, as in I hadn't seen police conducting their inquiries at the usual places. All the uncertainty could make for a more complicated day though, but it hadn't so far. I change the subject. 'Mate you heard of Buki Nneka?'

'Who?'

'Buki Nneka. Some Francophone sister, used to live in Hackney.'

'Hackney's a big place bruv. Why should I know her?'

'She sounds like she was a bit of a hustler and she's a 10!'

'I can't fuck them all, Challey!'

I laugh when I hear Klu doing the same.

'I ain't never heard of Bookey Knicker!' Klu stops laughing and is serious again, and says so, 'Bruv, serious. Mum wants to know, when are you coming to see her?'

FIVE MISSED CALLS... MERLEY

'I know.' I exhale, 'Tell her it has to be first thing tomorrow.'

Tomorrow.

I feel like I'm lying.

I have every intention of seeing her tomorrow but if there were a polygraph strapped to my fingers right now it would say I'm lying.

'It has to be today bruv. She's... insisting, like!' Klu says trying out a new word.

'I can't.'

'Why, what you on?'

'I've got to go see a horse about a dog out west.'

'West End?'

'Not West End. West London.'

Close to my apartment I pass the green Peugeot from this morning's excitement. The two men from the white roadside recovery van attend to the car, while flirting with a woman in a robe with the hood up. She might be the woman I spoke to earlier. As I walk to my flat I end the call with Klu but don't try to see the face of the hooded woman after I spot the Kelja tattoo on her wrist. The picture on the side of the white van is of a fat man with a big beard smiling about fixing any repairable car damage.

From inside the van the voice of a radio newsreader can be heard:

> *Police investigating the murder of two women whose bodies were discovered earlier today in the Brownswood area of Hackney say their appeal for information has provided them with potential leads and...*

At home I get changed into a jacket made of wool, cotton, and PVC. It is the finest in burglar chic with smooth running zips and spacious pockets. It's the kind of jacket that could have come with or without a hood but happens to come with a very special hood you can't see all the time. I wouldn't wear anything else to break into the house in the black-and-white photograph. I finish off with a diamond earring in my right ear. I wince but it's worth it to give potential witnesses something to fix on and report to the police in their statements. My piercing almost always threatens to close over in between the times I have occasion to put a ring through it. Then it's through and my fingertips only have a small speck of blood on them. They've seen worse.

I would feel much better having Klu with me for this next bit but it's going to call for stealth and calm. Klu lacks subtlety and is unpredictable.

I find the contact I'm looking for and the phone rings only once before it's picked up.

Driver

Fanny owns a lot of businesses in Green Lanes but he always has me meet him in his butcher's shop with its smell of clean and juicy death. I try not to read anything into it. I know how to do business and I don't think about what Fanny does to men who don't know how to do business. I prefer to be grateful he doesn't have me meet him at one of his Doner Kebab places.

On the stretch of Green Lanes called the High Road I stop and look at the statue of a fat six-foot-tall butcher with his head back mid-laugh and thick arms on his hips. From the blue trousers that aren't jeans and the red-and-white vertically striped apron he is the very image of a British tradesman. Except for the thick moustache he looks nothing like the Asians and Mediterraneans that Fanny has had working in here since the late 1980s.

As a kid I remember many butcher shops having one of these figures with a ruddy complexion outside and I was scared of all of them. My different foster mums would always laugh, not understanding what I had to be scared of... I did. A white man dressed as someone in the business of cutting dead flesh, standing stock still, laughing through rain, wind and snow. This one is very dented and chipped by all the elements London has to offer and not freshly painted like the similarly moustachioed figure on the side of the mechanics' van, but he is tougher. Whilst others like it have long been thrown out or melted down, here he stands hands on hips, shoulders back mid-laugh.

This one is the last man standing and I'm not afraid any more.

A fifty-year-old Turkish man with a scrubby beard and scruffy clothes hails me and holds the door open to the back of the store. Fanny leads me through corridors lined with boxes and equipment to his office. 'My boys are cleaning the car now.'

I smile as Fanny always has his boys cleaning cars.

'You're drinking pineapple juice – no ice, eh?' he says, and leaves me in the squalor to which I've become accustomed.

I had stopped guessing what Fanny and his gangsters spend their money on years ago but I can't help marvelling at what they don't spend their money on. Fanny makes the same amount of money as the average Premier League footballer. Include his legal business and he makes the money of the average Premier League footballer plus that of a promising English third division player too. But apart from Fanny's very nice line in luxury sports utility vehicles he shows nothing of his money – especially in his faded clothes.

Fanny also has a box marked Hospital Grade Clinical Mouthwash on the floor in the far corner of this office.

'Fanny has his girls gargle with that.' A familiar man stands in the doorway looking as unthreatening as a policeman can look in a vest and with a towel wrapped around his waist.

'Mr Roacher!'

'I'm twice blessed. We meet… morning and afternoon.'

Roacher is ebullient this time. He crosses the room and stands squarely at the window, blasé about me seeing him in an office above a sauna.

A policeman using a brothel is still a policeman.

'You're not here to sample Fanny's wares are you?' Roacher grins. 'What would the London community of boyz and mandem think if they knew, their hero, the great Nathan Mensah had to pay for sex?'

'I'm no one's hero Mr Roacher.'

'You wouldn't say that if you knew the number of boys we're getting here who are remaining silent?'

By here he means Stoke Newington Police Station which is fifteen minutes' walk from where the two of us are standing. I yearn for Fanny's return to break up the awkwardness. I'm glad I've taken off my burglar jacket and use my heel to move it under my seat.

'But the great Nate Mensah, when you talk – they listen. They're remaining silent, pleading entrapment, loop-holing the warrants. All on your say so! Why, just this morning the boys, our boys chased one of your boys all over Newham. They were positive he had something dodgy in his car. But by the time they caught up with him and could get reinforcements to where he'd abandoned his car he was remaining as silent as an Egyptian mummy except to say he had his lawyer on his phone telling him he could sue every policeman in Europe if we tried to open the boot to have a butcher's at what had him acting so uptight!' Roacher finishes his story and shakes his head, 'Newham probably won't get enough to hold him on, let alone charge him, the slippery sod!'

Roacher smiles his ugly smile, 'Just like a younger you, isn't that so Mensah? I wouldn't mind but these are not your black-history-month inventors you're keeping out of prison you know? They are little punks stabbing and shooting other little punks outside chicken shops.' Roacher changes tack. 'On the subject of social workers. You know who I've been thinking about today? Old Matthew Bright! You remember him don't you? He was in charge of that care home you used to live in back then. You had a little girlfriend in one of the other rooms didn't you? Asere Naynay Squirrelly?

'Naa Kworley,' I say.

'That's the girl! She accused Matthew Bright of raping her too didn't she? He beat the charges – what with it being a lot of problem girls' words against his and all that... soon after that beating he took.'

'I remember,' I say.

'Do you? Good. So do I,' Roacher affirms. He seems to be looking at the window and not through it.

'You know,' Roacher opines, 'social workers are like

priests. You always have to give them the benefit of the doubt, and assume that it's probably kids with a grudge trying to ruin 'em. But when one of 'em takes a grievous kicking, you're thinking there must have been some truth to the accusations. Emotional crime, Matthew wouldn't tell anybody what happened. Wouldn't even after his jaw got fixed – he couldn't say what happened, just muttered and stuttered. Your Monica used to have a monster temper on her, didn't she? But she didn't have the physical strength to do that to him. If she had been big enough, the silly bint could have stopped herself getting raped in the first place.'

Roacher keeps looking at the window, not even glancing my way. If I didn't know better I would think he wants me to heave him out of it.

'You used to have a temper on you too. Very quick to raise your fists in the schoolyard. That's why I had such high hopes for me and you but since you were eighteen, somewhere after Matthew Bright fell off Big Ben – you started being seen with a better class of criminal, like Fanny here and your temper disappeared and you've been as cool as the proverbial ever since! But I knew it was you, that did it for the girl, or for yourself. Either that, or all the girls jumped him, but no nails in the vicinity or scratches you'd expect if it were women. It would explain Bright's silence though. Shame, because of the girls.'

Roacher scratches his belly looming over his towel, thinking correctly that I won't lose any more respect for him.

'You know I went to see Matthew Bright in Devon. Devon mind you! And he was from Deptford! He'd already taken care of his own witness protection. I made it clear to him that the longer he waited the more difficult it would become to get you banged up for it. "Nathan Mensah can't get you," I told him.

But he didn't want to know. Can you believe it? A rapist like him scared like an ordinary citizen!' Roacher looks at me for the first time since he started talking. 'Yes I knew what he had done, I'm a copper after all and know the crimes those close to me are capable of.'

Roacher lets out a grunt or a laugh.

'What you did to him – the state he was in, you would have been better off killing him. I would have if it was my girlfriend he did that to. Think of that every time you wonder how you've stayed out of handcuffs for fifteen years on my watch.'

I don't comment.

Roacher looks at me hard, 'On a totally unrelated case – I want you to know, that goon of yours, the one whose mum took you in before you left care – Master Nii Klue Adjei, street name Klu? What's it called that you two are to each other? Foster cousins? Social brothers? I made sure that your boy got locked up for a humble like that. Not good for your street cred that you can't protect him… For the whole world to know you can be got at. Anyway, it is time that I'm off, duty calls,' Roacher smiles before asking, 'Oh by the way, what do you know about a new lot called The Shampoo Crew?'

I shake my head, making sure not to betray any surprise at hearing Klu's lead resurface here, now. Nodding and muttering something to himself with Devon in it, Roacher disappears.

I look around trying to think about anything other than what Roacher has just said.

'It's for the girls!' Fanny comes in. I must be looking at the box marked Hospital Grade Clinical Mouthwash in the corner in the same confused way I was when Roacher had walked in. 'Your car is ready.'

Fanny hands me a chilled glass of pineapple juice. He puts his hand on my shoulder. I try to stop myself tensing. It would be a shame if Fanny were to think I don't like him when I really do. I don't mind if he thinks that it's because I'm scared of him. He's a scary man. He's been my mentor in the crime game and taught me how to proceed in the right way. When I've finished my drink I follow Fanny outside to a private car park which has enough space for Grayson Fielding's helicopter to land in. There are some top of the range motors: a Range Rover with tinted windows, Mercedes Benz M class, Porsche Cayenne, an old model BMW X5, a new model BMW X5. All black. All clean.

'You heard any news about my son?' Fanny asks, speaking quickly.

'No.' I look around for the spectre of Roacher before putting on my burglar jacket, then at a still expectant Fanny, 'I've only asked around a bit you know.'

Fanny gives a sad nod.

I ask, 'Look, if you want me on it properly, full time...?'

'No, it's okay. I'm not sure if he wants to be found.'

'I'm serious man. No charge.' I zip up the jacket. It's not very cold but I'm trying not to think of Fanny and his son's sad story, but I go back to it, 'You've always helped me out with a car when I need one... I'll just...'

'No it's okay. He's a clever boy, educated at a good private school and a top university.'

I nod admiring the Range Rover that will soon be mine to drive. Fanny changes the subject. 'You're not like the other African gangsters. None of the jewellery, the big clothes, none of the...'

'I'm not a gangster Fanny, just an ordinary decent criminal.'

He looks at me with a who-are-you-kidding expression while I look back at the cars.

I don't know why Turkish hoods like working with Chelsea Tractors but they do. Nice ones.

'Which one do you want?'

'The Range Rover,' I repeat…

'Oh, to me they're all Range Rovers!'

I point at the Range Rover. It has the number plate ST0K3Y and big fuck-off black rims on the wheels.

'Okay, you take it,' he offers with his standard magnanimity, 'and don't bring it back here. When you finish today or tomorrow, you take it to my shop in Leyton.'

We look at each other silently for a moment.

When he shouts, one of his boys leaves a hose running and drives the car alongside us. I jump in to see that Fanny has already lost interest in me and his seventy thousand pound equipment loan. He trusts me I suppose.

I adjust my collar and put on gloves for the second time today, the ones I wore while I was being mistaken for an officer this morning.

Theft, going equipped for
Maximum penalty: 3 years imprisonment
Theft Act 1968, section 25

I manoeuvre the big car between Fanny's parking lot and the high street. Pausing, I look out at the world that doesn't want me. I take the number-plate-sized roll of paper from under my shirt and unroll it and prepare the adhesive I'll use to cover the current number plate. The cloned numbers look just as at home on the wrong Range Rover as they did on the correct vehicle parked in Shoreditch.

I don't mind if Fanny's people see. They'd understand me taking such precautions before I drive a car belonging to one of north-east London's biggest heroin wholesalers and distributors. But I do care if the grey Hyundai is around because I am as keen on him not following me as I am on the police not following me.

I pull out into Stoke Newington and look around for a Korean grey three-door car. I don't see one so I join the traffic heading west.

I play rap music at the highest volume the Range Rover can muster. I start with Busta Rhymes but switch to Jay-Z by Kensington for added arrogance.

If I can't do something without attracting attention it's better to attract lots of attention.

I always play rap music at maximum volume en route to committing a crime in west London. I've tried it with R&B but sometimes girls think it's for their benefit. With rap music – loud rap music mostly – everybody makes a point of not looking in my direction lest they legitimise my blatant attention seeking anti-social behaviour.

An hour's drive later I park the Range Rover five streets from the Chelsea address I'm headed to.

Cops are never fast enough to house break-ins

The house has a basement and two floors. I walk up the small flight of steps and knock on the door and get ready. No sound and no movement follows. I look around while I wait. Everybody hereabouts is gainfully employed or on holiday. The lock isn't all that but I struggle to pick it.

I realise what the problem is. My hand. It's not that the watch around it says it's 1.18 pm but that it's shaking. I'm disgusted. If my body reacts badly to a nothing crime like this one, how can I expect to be taken seriously when the real shit is going down? I'm forced to lean back and look as I insert the three-pronged paper-clip sized lock breaker. It's only a standard lock. It stands no chance. I recoil as the door opens, look around for an alarm box and don't see one. It doesn't matter. Silent alarm or not, I'll be long gone by the time the police or private contractors arrive.

Burglary in a dwelling /Breaking and entering
Maximum penalty: 14 years imprisonment.
Theft Act 1968, Section 9

I walk in like somebody who belongs in south-west London. A painting, of what look like bubbles in outer space, hangs in the hall. It looks expensive.

Once in I take a look around. I'm good at this kind of thing. I've never belonged anywhere and that somehow means that I can take a look at other people and figure out where they belong. The same applies to houses and figuring out who should live in them.

The kitchen is the neglected area in breaking and entering. Spices, pots, pans and a clock have a poor resale value. It's still 1.18 pm. On the wall is a canvas painting of the same kind as in the hall but it has different bubbles. An iPod flashes a low battery signal at me when I look it over. Two sounds break the silence at the same time, the MP3 player's low battery whimper and a car engine outside.

I shake tins and jars in the cupboard. There's food sloshing sounds inside most of them or no sound but they are the right weight. I suppose people in this part of town wouldn't store cash in fake baked bean tins. Money is more likely to be behind portraits but I'm not looking for money, am I? I'm not a burglar today but I still check the hall and the doorways of the rooms for laser lenses.

The biggest room has been converted into a bedroom.

It and the next room are straight out of a Swedish furniture showroom. It's lived in but it's like the residents don't want to make it too comfortable in case they're put off trying to get ahead in the world.

I quickly move onto the third room. This room belongs to an African woman. This is her room. As soon as I walk in I'm encircled by the smell of all the things Black women put in their hair, or on their faces and bodies. The warm air smells of Pinky© hair lotion and the once hot combs are long since cooled. Buki has been here and this is the room where she lived. It wasn't for long or else she didn't use as much of these products as the girls I had grown up with. It's how Monica's room used to smell and maybe like something my mother would have used, but I wouldn't really know. But I do know Buki doesn't seem to have left anything much for me to find.

I look up at the low ceiling and the tiles there. I jump and punch at the tile above me. The reinforced polystyrene disappears. I jump up again, and hanging off the beam, stick my head through the square hole.

In the pitch black I can only see about a foot in front of me in any direction. I make a pop sound with my lips and listen. My radar tells me it's not big enough to be an attic but enough to hide contraband from lazy seekers. I can't identify the sound I hear outside or if I've heard it before but when I hear it this time I get a sharp pain in the heart and fall to the floor. I lie with my mouth open taking in no air but trying to think about what to do and who to call about the numbing tremor in my chest. The sound, whatever it was has gone away, then I realise that I'm not having a heart attack. It's my phone vibrating.

SEVEN MISSED CALLS... MERLEY

Swearing quietly, I pick myself up off the floor and look at the empty room and the ceiling above it with fresh eyes.

I'm at least a foot taller than Buki's given height in her passport so I'm thinking that if Buki Nneka's stowed anything up there it would be above the bed or the small couch in the corner next to the window. I jump up knocking at tiles. One by one they move out of place and come back to rest lopsided and haphazardly or sometimes disappear behind another tile to be disturbed again later. Forensic officers will love the dust particles found on my head and shoulders which are like a kind of dynamic dandruff. Directly above the foot of the bed I knock at a tile which doesn't move.

I try again. Solid.

Again, harder than before and it remains even more resolute.

I smile.

Hoisting myself into the darkness for the second time near the immobile tile I hang silently except for my breathing, and my eyes alight on a heavy object, its bulk spread across where four ceiling beams meet.

It's not a body. Ceiling beams in a house can't hold the weight of a body, so it's not that in an old brown suitcase.

After some delicate and muscled manoeuvrings I bring it down, put it on the bed and get my breath back. Now I have a suitcase which was hidden above the ceiling. I look at my watch. I've spent two and a half of the five minutes I've given myself to get in and out of here, shaking tins and looking in empty rooms.

The suitcase still has the name tag on the handle. Most people do not fill this in but she did. It doesn't say much but still tells me a lot.

NAME: Buki Nneka
FROM: Darfur, Sudan
TO:_____

Maybe London is not where she wanted to go or where she had been planning to go. When she was coming from Sudan she was far from the It girl she tried to become, or did become. A named suitcase belongs to somebody with nothing to hide or no reason to impress. It's a Samsonite bag but an old model perhaps from the seventies or eighties with a chrome effect. Quality, and top of the range in its day but this wasn't its day. Did Buki inherit this from an older relative or did some salesman carry it to Sudan thirty or forty years ago where it lay unmolested in some depot until Miss Nneka acquired it?

I open the suitcase and I'm hit by the smell of camphor. I picture the fresh-off-the-plane girl Buki was when she blinked her way into London. I quickly rifle through her clothes. Dresses, blouses and skirts – maybe a dozen outfits in total. One yellow raincoat. She'd been told about London rain but she hadn't been told nobody wears a yellow raincoat. I feel sleazy enough so I don't hang around looking through the large pocket of underwear after a cursory inspection reveals there's nothing in there but lace. Everything in the suitcase would fit Buki Nneka.

I'm not as good with women's clothes as I should be but this stuff doesn't look expensive. A lot of the brighter coloured blouses don't have labels. Handmade but not Champs-Elysées or Milano handmade. Third-world-township handmade. Everything is folded so meticulously. I wouldn't be surprised if Buki only ever opened this suitcase to retrieve extra money she maybe had stored in one of its many compartments, but turned her back on its contents and her past forever.

Buki Nneka doesn't want any of her London friends to know the third-world-township Buki Nneka and she doesn't want to be reminded, but she's kept the suitcase. Just like she kept renewing her lease at the business unit she had left behind.

It's like Buki knew her dream would one day be over and when she had to go back to the real world it would be with this.

I pick up a small blue box I hadn't noticed before. It's a little box cynically designed to pull on the strings of people that have hearts. It's corny unlike this house. The box means absolutely nothing to me but I can tell it means something to somebody. Too much hassle to fold notes into. It could hold a Yale key or two. It doesn't but it's covered with glitter. If this thing was in the house it belonged to, it would be in a cottage in Somerset and would not be my problem.

I stand holding it in the hall, pondering which of the rooms to check next. I'm not confident about finding anything more in here. I had high hopes for this place and I thought I'd left the best for last. It had jumped out at me in the file Fielding gave me. Buki's sanctuary from her husband. Still holding the blue box I move on, heading for the door. I've taken in a lot today. I will go home now, chill out and cogitate. I might have missed a link, or someone that might lead to a link.

Just then, I hear loud voices at the door, five metres of hall away. I freeze.

Revenge of the routine check!

There's a big sound that might have been a loud knock but the front door opens. I see a flash of yellow and black and I unfreeze, dashing into a bathroom. CID and uniformed police. My heart's beating. I force myself to calm down. Now I'm grateful to the blue box for delaying me from heading for that front door earlier to greet the police. I pocket it.

I had somewhat unconsciously clocked this room as one of the two ways out of the house apart from the front door but I'm only here because it was the closest – not because I'm the most professional. The window is smaller than the one in the bedrooms and it faces out onto the front of the house.

I ask myself if there's any chance the police won't check in here. I hold my ear as close to the door as I can so I've still got reaction time if one of them puts a boot to it. This is serious. I rush to the window, its large enough for me to squeeze through if it opens all the way out. It does. There's a lone police officer outside wearing a yellow high-visibility jacket. He's standing on sentry duty, hands behind his back, looking around at nothing in particular. At best I might have four seconds to get this window open, squeeze through it and jump down, drop and roll, without being seen or heard by the police, then choose a direction and run. Four seconds won't be enough and the officer would tell me so except he hasn't seen me, because I haven't jumped yet.

Still hoping I can get out of this unscathed I creep back towards the door. I listen again. I hear the police talking amongst themselves. They must be working through the house room by room.

They haven't been called here for me, I tell myself, but they will find me just the same. I have absolutely no explanation that they might consider for not locking me up. I can't have any more than twenty seconds before this door is barged open.

I have to run.

I let my heart race some more. Adrenaline is always a friend when running from the police in a strange place.

Fingers trembling I take my phone out and type a short message.

'WEST ON WHITE MOTORBIKE.'

I'm shaking all over as I stash the phone. I push the window open and climb out as quickly and as cautiously as I can.

'Oi!' the officer below sees me, 'Stop, police!'

Of course I don't stop, but jump.

Resisting arrest
Maximum Penalty – 2 years imprisonment and/or a fine
Police Act 1964, section 51

Rolling after I land uninjured, I choose to go left, the opposite direction to where my car is waiting and closer to where there might be more police at the front entrance of the house.

'Stop! Police!'

I still don't stop.

I run and vault over fences and walls dividing backyards. The officer runs parallel keeping an eye on me all the while. This is too easy for him. While I'm jumping over unpredictable and unwieldy front lawn obstacles to my freedom the officer hasn't got so much as a cracked west London paving stone to stop him from keeping up and surely figuring out a way to bridge the gap and tackle me and send me to jail for years.

I feel like a race horse being barracked by someone that has put a bet on me. I look up and see one last fence before the road. I calculate that I'll get over that and the officer will round the corner and be two metres behind me maximum. That's tackling distance for a rugby player. I should be able to open it to twenty metres which would be enough if this was Hackney.

But I don't know anybody out here. If the officer is faster than the average white man I may not even manage that. He might stay with me barking street names until his friends from the K-9 unit arrive. My heart threatens to explode in my chest as I haul myself over the last fence, throwing myself to the lions. I land better than expected and the officer who should be rounding the corner nearest me is moving slightly slower than I feared.

I snap out the hood velcroed to the inside of the back of

my jacket. It makes a loud zipping noise as I pull it up over my head like a diver's helmet. It comes down over my face with a breathing grille which is mostly for show. I put the big Commando-style goggle lenses over my eyes and then flex my gloved fists. I hear him before I see him.

'*...Am in foot pursuit of an IC3 male, approx six feet two, thirty years of age... running west on...*'

He comes around the corner baton first. I grab him by the arm and steer him into my waiting knee. I hit him in the soft part of his belly. My knee is calloused like everybody else's but the soft part of the belly isn't as soft as it should have been. He's suitably winded but he doesn't want to fall on the floor. Double-fisted and judo-style I hit him in the face and he goes down.

Assault with intent to resist arrest
Maximum Penalty: 2 years imprisonment and/or unlimited fine
Offences Against the Person Act 1861, section 38

We both ignore the calls over his radio to confirm his location. I'm kicking him and he tries to fend me off and get up. His yellow fluorescent jacket falls open, strapped to his bullet-proof vest is a gun. I can't be sure if he's reaching for it or if his hands are just flailing when I quickly step towards him and take it from him. This is good because I have to hit him less. He stops resisting so I stop kicking. He puts both his hands up as I admire the new semi-automatic. I put the baton in my belt and kick the back of his knee. I put him in a suppressing headlock.

It's essential I don't say anything to him. If this is the most traumatic thing that's ever happened to him in his career he might remember the sound of my voice for the rest of his life. I'm not even keen on him hearing the pattern of my breathing but I can't help that as I hold his head in the crook of my arm.

I press his gun to his head and I hold my phone in front of his face. He reads my phone's display:

'*WEST ON WHITE MOTORBIKE.* '

He understands. He shakes his head. I press the gun harder into his head and still he refuses, shaking his head as determinedly as before, I put the phone back in my pocket releasing my hold on the officer. Still on his knees he turns around to face me. Keeping the gun trained on him I slide the safety mechanism off with my free hand then contract my trigger finger. Armed police only get called out for the kind of criminal stupid enough to shoot police officers. I hope this one thinks I'm that kind of stupid...

My breath is starting to fog up the eyeholes, hopefully scaring him more although messing with my visibility. I can't know what he sees but he must be scared. He should be because I'm tired, angry and might just shoot him.

He grips his radio and says:

'*Suspect heading west on a white motorbike. I repeat suspect heading west on a white motorbike, over!*'

I nod at him, satisfied my bluff has worked. I rip his shoulder radio off, take its battery out and shove it in his mouth. I leave him handcuffed to a fence and run, moving fast. I throw the officer's gun and the remains of the radio onto the back seat of their car, but I keep the baton. I lent my last one to Klu and he hasn't returned it. The car reminds me of my old BMW but in police colours. Stoked up with adrenaline I'm tempted to steal it, but I'm not seventeen any more. I have my own waiting getaway vehicle and all these pandas probably have aggressive new global positioning technology that lock thieves in and drive them to the nearest cop shop for safekeeping. Releasing the zip on my hood so

I can breathe better I slow down and walk to my wheels, trying to give the impression I'm not in a hurry. I don't see police back-up, a jogger, dog walker or a twitching curtain.

I've taken off my jacket when I begin to hear the sirens of police cars on their way to help in search of an IC3 suspect proceeding west on a white motorbike. This IC3 male heads east in a black Range Rover.

Hēh! Mī ŋyē yē bīēē!

I am at the Walthamstow end of the A406 before I realise I've forgotten to play loud rap music.

I get to Fanny's shop on Leytonstone High Street, outside it a seated Turkish gentleman sips from a small cup with his legs folded as he reads from a newspaper. I tap on the horn gently three-and-a-half times. He doesn't tense or turn so the only way I know he's heard me is that he softly places his cup down on the light stainless steel table, then looks not at me but back the way I've come to make sure I haven't arrived with a police pursuit team.

Fanny's younger brother is happy with what he has and hasn't seen and he coughs an order into the smoky shop with shisha bongs lining the window.

A minute later another Turkish gentleman, unseen, pulls open the gate at the side of the building. I drive in, relieved to be off road, and I park in the far corner. Making sure I've left nothing inside I take the jacket off and throw it in an oil drum, where later it will be burnt. I strip off the dummied-up number plates and add those to the oil drum. The gate has been closed and locked behind me so I take a side door into the building. It's exactly the kind of place I would have looked for to take refuge in forty-five minutes ago if I'd had the luxury of being chased in east London instead of in the unfamiliar west.

There's only a slightly discernible break in the conversation as I walk back outside past the men and their cigarettes and small cups.

Fanny's brother is still alone and reading his newspaper. He's taller, bigger-built and seems at least twenty years younger than Fanny. I place the key on the table in front of him. He clears his throat and with one hand adjusting the peak of his hat he silently places his saucer over it, never taking his eye off the paper or looking at me.

ONE MISSED CALL... MERLEY

Thirty minutes later, running across Hackney Marshes I fix a bluetooth earpiece around my jogging ear and dial a friend. I end the call, dial her again, end the call, and dial her again.

CALLING MONICA...

Monica Asere, formerly known as Naa Kworley Asere is looking at her handset right now as it tells her it's an unfamiliar number but at the same time knowing exactly who it is who's calling, and she's cursing. She'll be putting her cigarette out first, and lighting a new one.

'Mensah,' she hums.

'Asere,' I pant.

'Nigga!' Monica sounds aghast, 'Are you calling me while you're fuckin'?'

'No!' I try to regulate my breathing as I run across the marshes. Eighty-eight football pitches and I've got to cross most of them.

'Are you running from the police then?'

'Kind of...'

'That's alright then.' She makes settling down noises, 'I heard you killed two women yesterday.'

'And you believed it?'

I deny it like somebody whose respiration is at a premium

right now.

I hear her shrug, 'If you did, I know you had your reasons.'

I'm not in position to marvel at what a woman Monica is right now with her disrespect that belies her expertise in all matters bureaucratic and legal. 'Listen. Do you remember a police officer named Roacher?'

While Monica is silent, there's just the sound I make running over grass and jumping over shit, and dodging under goal posts.

'I've seen him twice today... Roacher. He's asking about Matthew Bright... I don't like those kinds of coincidences.'

'There's a friend of mine in town... if you need to disappear Nathan.' Monica is one of the few people who still calls me Nathan. 'He can get people in and out of the country like it's nothing. Don't tell him I sent you but he'll be getting a new haircut tonight.' Monica adds, 'If you need me just call.'

But I know that without her needing to say it. I can't find words to describe what Monica is to me except that she's everything Klu isn't and a little bit of what Aunty Merley is. For the rest of my jog home I am able to coerce some life into the iPod I took from the house in Chelsea.

I don't know why I took the blue box but I had to steal the iPod.

Theft, in a dwelling
Maximum Penalty: 7 years imprisonment
Theft Act 1968, section 1

One can get a lot from an iPod, but not cash in any amount that would interest me. It's not stealing when I don't intend to keep the thing or sell it on. It's technically stealing but when the police do it, to inspect and/or listen to the contents like I am doing, it's called evidence gathering.

There's some pop music of the typical three and a half minutes kind and African music of the fifteen minute variety. The quantity of tracks matches the newness. There's a song by an unnamed artist titled The Key. I smile. I could do with one of those right now.

I scroll genres looking for some kind of music I wouldn't be expecting a first generation immigrant woman from north-east Africa to listen to. No classical, jazz, samba or trance music. There's one track that gets my attention, it has no name of artist or composer or song track either, and is very short. I press play and hear an angry distorted voice speak:

'Listen Bitch! You are going to die! You don't do what you're told and you talk too fuckin' much!'

There is no more singing, I put my head down and get ready to run the five kilometres into Hackney proper.

You eat off the plate all you want but not Nate!

I leave the spoils of today's campaign in the centre of my gaff's main space as I discover that I'm very hungry and that my cupboards and fridge have no provisions apart from bread that passed its sell-by date three days ago. I throw some corned beef between four slices of the bread, add some Ghanaian black pepper, onions and Maggi® sauce. I dust off the sandwich toaster in the hope it will kill the last of the germs from the mould. I have also run out of milk so I will drink my tea black with extra sugar.

I'm not eating like somebody who stowed one hundred and twenty-five thousand pounds in a safety deposit box this morning.

I eat my repast at the coffee table and look at the iPod that

I'm now charging.

I meditate on what I've seen and heard today. Finding the iPod with the death threat on it really isn't that helpful because this might not belong to Buki Nneka. But then the police had been called to the house, armed. For me?

Over four hours looking for her and I have nothing else to show for my time. I am no closer to figuring out where Buki is. I still wait on Lauriston's report on the fingerprint analysis from the Stratford business centre. If that produces nothing, I'll have nothing, the same nothing which lead me to break into the Chelsea place. On top of everything I believe I've got a reasonable-sized headache caused by re-opening my ear piercing.

I'm not aware of falling asleep but when the over-active use of my door buzzer rudely wakes me I am sprawled on the sofa. I look for my fourth gun and skulk towards my front door.

I switch on my security monitor. A man standing outside my door is stooped over, just out of shot, looks like he is breaking in. When the man adjusts his hood to cool himself down after his exertions I recognise the shape of his head. Quickly I flick the locks on my side of the door and swing it open, 'Feel free,' I say, with what I hope is a heavily sarcastic tone. I ignore the intruder and look at the locks he was trying to breach.

'Oi,' he exclaims as if he's surprised to see me at my own front door.

'Wassup?' I respond.

'So what, I can't come in yeah?' he asks.

I shrug.

Klu smiles and knocks an open but heavy palm against my stomach, 'What have you been doing with the day?'

Then quickly he moves into my flat. I check the corridor

behind him is empty. Klu is doing the same with the interior.

'Staying alive.' I see my phone has logged a missed call from Klu and three more from his mother.

'This is all you've got?' He holds a bag which is a quarter-full of white powder and waves it at me accusingly. It has GARI on the front surrounded by a Taj-Mahal-type design, 'You?'

Klu offers me some, pouring some of the dried cassava in my cupped hand. I thresh the ready to eat staple in my palm and funnel it into my mouth.

Klu smacks his lips, 'Have you got anything to drink then?'

He opens the fridge. It is even emptier than when I'd opted for the insufficient lunch of tea and a mouldy-bread sandwich.

'Champs!' Klu shouts, pulling out a bottle of champagne from one of the eye-level cabinets with a see-through door. 'Call this my coming home toast!'

I don't drink champagne so probably his sister Dedei left it behind after a club promotion event. She's used my place as an after-after-party spot a few times because she considers it smart.

Klu rinses a glass and fills it with sparkling yellow-green bubbles. With his right hand he passes it to me, and holding the bottle by it's neck with his left, aims it at his lips.

Putting my glass of champagne down untouched, I wait to learn the purpose of his visit.

Klu savours the champagne. 'This place don't change much does it? You haven't painted or nothing! It still looks like the old Hackney hospital or factory or whatever it was.'

'A school,' I say and return to the sofa I had fallen asleep on.

'Yeah,' Klu shakes his head, 'you bought a flat in a building that used to be your school, 's fucked up!'

'I liked school.' I shrug, 'You knew who everybody was. The good guys, the bad guys, everybody in between. There was something really honest there. People were shallow about who their friends were and they didn't pretend otherwise about their shallow reasons. There was no need to be any other way.'

'I was a bully at my school,' Klu reminisces.

'And I was bullied. But they were all my size. Even when there were more of them, they were all my size. There was something really honest about being bullied at school.'

'Your view is nice though.'

'Yeah? Helps with spotting the gangsters I suppose.'

'The term they use in prison is negatively affiliated youth group,' Klu corrects me.

My mobile phone rings. The fire-alarm ringtone is Lauriston.

'Can you talk?' Lauriston greets me.

I look at Klu aiming the balled up empty GARI bag at a bin. The plastic expands as it flies through the air but it lands in the bin without touching its sides. Klu makes a gun of his hand, and blows on his index and middle finger, the gun barrel.

'Yeah,' I tell Lauriston.

'I've got the results for the prints.'

'Of course you have.'

He takes the compliment in his stride like a good yuppie, 'I made out fingerprints belonging to five different people. One of them has a record for very minor things. Then three have Amnesty International type records. Violence at demonstrations, breaking into animal labs, assaulting rich chicks wearing fur... you know the type.'

I do.

He continues, 'I'm about to send you the bumf on all these jokers by secure email but straight off the bat I know who you'll be visiting. Hector Edmondson! You're really going to like this guy. A multiple loser... possession, petty burglary, shoplifting, mugging. He's never served a proper jail-term but he's always in and out and he's out on bail at the moment. No permanent place of abode but he's given an address in Aldgate more than once. You two are going to be friends. Play nicely now! Oh and for a bonus, have you heard, hot off the press that Roacher is dead?'

'What? DCI Roacher?' I watch Klu turn to look at me now, taking a keen interest in my conversation, 'Out of Stoke Newington?' I ask, wanting confirmation.

'Yep. Well actually he lived in Southend. Can you believe it? You'd think a man that lived in Southend would have a sunnier disposition. Maybe it was that long drive every day. They found him dead some hours ago. Locked garage, note, plastic tube from the exhaust into his Jag.'

Not knowing if this is good news or bad or neither we say nothing for a while.

'The Shampoo Crew,' I mutter to myself.

'What?' Lauriston says.

'We'll talk later.' I sign off.

'Roacher is dead,' I tell Klu. And head for the shower.

The last thing Roacher asked me two hours ago was if I had heard of The Shampoo Crew.

Why didn't they ask Adjei?

After showering I replace the streetwear with a black suit. Klu has his back to me, sitting on the armrest of my sofa. His feet buried in the part of the furniture his arse should be on. His left hand plays with the knuckles on his right. His expression is like a baby predator in a wildlife documentary, up on it's haunches almost accidentally in a pre-strike pose, vaguely aware that he should be attacking his prey, but unsure whether to use his claws or teeth.

He has a beard of particularly tough hair he has to shave every day. He scratches his chin now and there's a crackling sound. Klu growls quietly to himself and slides down to the cushion part of the sofa. I thought he was ready to say what brought him here but instead he picks up the stolen iPod I've left out on the coffee table.

'I didn't think Nate Mensah would like The Key!'

'What?' I ask examining the buttons on my shirt.

'Her!' He holds the iPod's display screen up at me. 'The Key.' There is a picture of the same woman in the passport picture Fielding gave me this morning, right there in the image window of a song playing on the MP3 player. 'That's Buki Nneka,' I say to Klu, 'you said you didn't know her?'

'I don't know no Boogey Nekka! I know The Key though! She was on The House one of those reality tv shows. 'She is buff to bumber! Wait, let me get her Facebook page.' Klu is as casual as anything as if he hasn't just found the biggest development in this case of mine all day.

'Facebook?' I say dumbstruck. There she is – a picture of The Key, the staged alias of a woman whose whereabouts I have been pursuing all day. Instead of the passport and respectable photos with her husband here she is in a club holding a glass of champagne. There is a wealth of information here about this woman. All this while I've been scraping around on an iPod that may not be hers for the littlest indicator, and here is page after page of comments from people who love her, or don't like her, and telling where she might be.

Fielding didn't tell me any of this. Musical aspirations and self-promotion in a big way, a reality tv show cancelled after less than a fortnight on air. There is no mention or sight on Facebook of Grayson Fielding or Buki Nneka's real name.

Klu flips through web pages and web pages of Buki, The Key, Nneka and a lot of them picture her closer to Patrick Fitz than he had been prepared to admit. Pictures can lie, but Patrick Fitz definitely did.

What possible motive might a record label have in making... or helping Buki disappear? If she was big enough for a disappearing act to make her sell more music, even I would have heard of her. The Key's face is heavily made up and her hairstyle is far more elaborate than in her passport photo and in the formal photos Fielding has of her.

Before anything else, I should first see what the Lauriston's multiple loser has to offer.

I put a black tie on.

'You've got to come and see my mum,' Klu says. Klu has stopped helping.

I say, 'Not today.' Today I am chasing around London, impersonating and attacking police officers, and shaking down the bad men for information. It isn't the day for seeing Klu's mum. 'Tomorrow,' I say.

'It has to be today.'

'Klu!'

Then Klu is in front of me, stopping me.

'It has to be today.'

I forget what I'm saying. He knows exactly what he will do to me if this conversation doesn't go right.

I have always thought we would fight one day. It's inevitable. Unlike me he lacks balance. We like spending our money on different things and we like getting it different ways. The play-fights we've had before were like training for all the fights we were going to have with others but the real fight itself is still to come.

I should be able to beat him. I am older but not old, taller and I don't lose when I fight. Klu is stockier, packs a harder punch and he has lost more fights than I have been in because I fight when I have to but he fights for a laugh and for something to do. I don't think he feels pain. I feel pain but I do not show it.

'Alright we'll go,' I back down. We will fight one day but not when I have a brand new suit, shirt and tie on.

'We'll go?' Klu's expression doesn't change.

'We'll go.'

Klu finally softens but he's still stern, ready to escort me outside.

Things to do in Hackney when you're not dead...

Klu looks straight ahead in the driver's seat of his orange Ford Focus. If this was the eighties it would have been a Ford Capri.

'So they got Roacher?' Klu makes a friendly conversation opener.

'He got himself, Lauriston said,' I reply.

I sit beside Klu in the passenger seat and put my seatbelt on, for real.

'This doesn't make any sense,' I say, then leave a pause so that Klu will think I'm talking about having to see his mother on the kind of day I'm having. Then I tell him what really doesn't make any sense. 'This random guy in the City wants me to find his woman who's gone missing.'

'This is the Bougie Nexus ting?' Klu asks.

'Yeah. She ain't left him, he says. She's missing he says. But he doesn't tell me she's this wannabe singer with a Facebook profile with five fucking thousand friends. He doesn't tell me there's something up with a house out west she used to live in, that it looks like everybody has cleared out of.'

'It's simple,' Klu says, 'he didn't want to prejudice your search.'

'What?' I ask distracted, as I adjust the left-hand-side mirror so I can see what's behind us.

'The Facebook thing ain't all that anyway. Every mutha-fucka on there's a liar. They only use certain pictures of themselves, they play like they're happier than they are or angrier or smarter or deeper when they ain't!' Klu pauses. 'This guy wants you to find his woman and not be confused by all the other bullshit.'

Klu jumps out of the car and I follow. His tutorial continues over the indiscreet bright orange roof. 'It's like when I had my trial. My brief made sure that the jury didn't know about any of my previous or my known associates. If that jury had heard about my arrests for assault and going equipped and that I hung out with cats like you…' Klu points his index finger at me which is rude '…they might've thought I was a badder bad man than what I am. They would 'ave locked me up for longer than a six to twelve, trust.'

I nod and we walk towards an African cafe-restaurant with Merley's Kitchen written in chalk on the sign outside. Klu was making sense, but he wasn't finished. 'Or you know what? It could be she's the one who's real and he's the bullshitter and he don't want you to find her at all.'

'Hi bossman!' Inside Merley's kitchen a beautiful Black woman greets me without taking a mobile phone away from her ear.

'Hello Dedei.' Dedei is Klu's older sister and the baby she is holding is Klu's son. She's wearing incredibly expensive designer clothes engineered to look cheap.

I take her hand as I pass and kiss it. Dedei simpers politely and I move on toward the eatery's main counter. Klu's mother Aunty Merley is there. If I can keep this to ten minutes it won't upset the balance of my day too much.

Aunty Merley is a five-foot-five pear-shaped woman and owner, proprietor and chief of this African establishment. When I change my phone and phone number I list her with my provider as one of the people to forward my new number to.

She is one of the few people that has constant access to me and of the few she is the only one who abuses it.

'Aunty!' I call to her.

She raises her palm at me signalling that I sit. I frown at her and point at my wrist. She looks at me and my watch with disdain but then the sour look goes away and she turns with a big smile to a white woman behind me. 'What can I get for you lovely lady?'

I glare at the lovely lady who nervously steps around me, and hesitates before making her order. I look her up and down from her collarless blouse and tie-and-dye skirt to her brightly coloured rubber shoes. Lovely lady stutters at me then at Aunty Merley who still looks warmly at her and ignores me. Something's wrong if lovely lady is about to get what she wants from Aunty Merley ahead of me. I turn my attention back to the middle-aged African patron.

'What can I get for you?' Aunty Merley asks lovely lady.

Aunty Merley is being stubborn. I look around for Klu and swear when I see he has disappeared. It's a fact, African women are the worst practitioners of customer service. They can't help it. It's their nature. Back in Africa they only cooked for their husband and children.

Aunty Merley's rudeness is legendary around here. But she

has chosen now to act like she cares about her customers.

She is making a point. The sooner I sit down the quicker I can simulate having learnt whatever lesson I'm being taught. I shoot my cuffs and go on and sit down at Dedei's table.

I glare at Aunty Merley and listen to the mock dramatic story Dedei tells into her phone. She and the baby look at me with passing curiosity but no break in the narrative or the child's play.

Dedei is a genuinely good girl who looks like Klu but not spookily so. As a proxy older brother I helped to guide her through her teenage years but they passed by with a minimum of fuss. She had no difficulty in rejecting the east London invitations to impregnate her and seemed to take no notice of this world until it offered something she wanted. She floated through her exams and then to everyone's surprise she started her party-promotion business. Dedei expects the best and the world has tried not to disappoint her. Except today. Today she is pissed off.

'…And you know everybody's out there these times, DJs, soundboys, MCs, street teams. Then I got the text from Lorna saying she was really sick and could I come and see her. I try calling her but she doesn't pick up and you know she never checks her Facebook page!' Dedei is saying, 'So I went up there and…'

The baby is getting in her way and with a start she propels him towards me, 'Addy, go to Uncle Nate.'

'No,' I shake my head at Klu II, 'Stay with Aunty Dedei.'

I lose again, and from my lap the little boy looks at me. For a second I almost transfer my annoyance to him for me being here and not getting on with finding Buki Nneka.

'Get me a pineapple juice then,' I tell Dedei.

'The ice machine's broke,' she warns.

'Good,' I glance at her shapely bottom as she walks away. I transfer little Nii-Addy to my left thigh. I produce my phone and scan through the internet. I don't like using my phone data because of police-surveillance tracing and the like but this café already definitely registers as one of my known locations.

My sense of being overwhelmed at the amount of information at my fingertips fades quite quickly when I realise it is mostly all fluff like Klu has warned. There are hundreds of pictures of Buki with the small club promoter logos. These photos do lie. I could find every single one of the hundreds of people Buki has been pictured beside and there's no guarantee any one of them could tell me one thing about who she really is and where I could find her right now.

The most interesting part of the Facebook profile page is the status. The media greatly enjoys when criminals forget themselves or underestimate the snitches they had on their friends list and use their status to assist various law enforcement agencies to relocate them to Her Majesty's Pleasure.

Buki Nneka has been updating her status three or four times a day until about four days ago. I mentally revise places in order of relevance to music. Throughout the profile, still no reference or any picture of Grayson Fielding.

Some of Buki's pictures do however provide a lead. Three weeks ago she had posted a series of five pictures showing the stages of a tattoo she was having. The tattoo was of a key, a beautiful key. It would be unwieldy to handle but whatever it opened would be worth it.

Suddenly the phone is being grabbed. I grab it back before baby Addy can put it in his mouth. I taunt him with it and put it away. I've got enough to think about for now.

I jiggle Addy around like I've seen other people do with babies, 'Ay Addy. Wassup?' The baby's frown turns into a smile. For him everything is up.

'Ay!' I smile putting my hand straight, palm up in front of him. The baby claps me on it.

Dedei has finished on the phone and retrieves the baby from me replacing him with a glass of pineapple juice. I look over to Aunty Merley. She is serving the third person to have walked in here after I did.

'Did you get all that?' Dedei waves her phone at me.

'Yes.'

Aunty Merley passes with plates of food for some of her customers. I look at her trying not to scowl.

'I'm so sorry about yesterday,' Dedei says to me. 'I had to go to Milton Keynes... Today I was supposed to be going on holiday with that new friend of mine Angelica, one of the Polish girls that worked here last year.'

Aunty Merley keeps a steady stream of east European girls working here. She allays any guilt or confusion about having white waitresses in an African eatery by dressing them up in traditional kente skirts and headwraps.

'You remember Lorna Palmer don't you?'

'Uhmmm...'

'Yeah you do! She never lets us forget she's one of your conquests.' Dedei kisses her teeth. 'I thought she was in hospital or something! I had to drive up there.'

'So what was up with her?' I sigh heavily and lean back.

'She was fine! She doesn't know how I got that text or who sent it. The whole thing must have been some dumb pointless hoax. Now Angelica's not picking up her phone and we're supposed to be leaving today.' Baby Addy is falling asleep in her arms. So she whispers now, 'I can't believe I'm stuck in Hackney! I should be on a beach or on an island full of beautiful, rich people. Hackney? There's nobody here!'

She is exaggerating. I know there are people here because I've seen them here. Some of them are even getting killed here. I look over at Aunty Merley. She isn't looking this way and her customer service is getting even more conscientious.

'Which island was this friend going to take you to?' I surprise Dedei by taking an interest. 'You know... Mallorca, Ibiza, all them party islands... Did she tell you which one you were going to first?'

'I don't know, but it doesn't matter... can I ask you something?'

This is not going to be a good thing.

'You're a gangster aren't you?'

'Nope,' I tap my fingers on the table. 'And I don't know why you keep asking me that.'

She tells me why, 'You've got these businesses you don't care about. You pay me too much to be a manager in the shop. My friends think you're only using it as a money-laundering front.'

'I wouldn't do that to you, even if I was a gangster.'

'You know what else makes me think you are?' She doesn't pretend to wait for my go ahead, 'Klu respects you. And, remember a couple of years ago when mum nearly lost this place because they raised the rates and bailiffs started coming around?'

Dedei used they in the same way her brother did, to describe agencies in authority.

She continues, 'You know what I heard? A Black man went to the owner of the bailiff company and threatened him.' Dedei looks around before reducing the volume of her whisper further, 'With a gun... and told him to leave the shop in Kingsland Square alone. Except this Black man didn't tell the bailiff which shop to leave alone so that's why the shops around here got a pass on having to pay anything until it was time for contract renewals. Threatened his whole family too they said. My mum saved loads of money – fixed up this place a bit.'

'I remember that.'

'You do.'

Nodding, 'I remember, my shop…'

'Our shop!' Dedei interrupts.

'Our shop was the only place that kept paying what I – we owed. Remember that? I've got the receipts to prove it. What do I need to go putting guns in people's faces when I could pay my bills? No bailiffs were coming to visit us.'

Dedei and I stare at each other until Aunty Merley finally comes and sits down. I hadn't yet resigned myself to being trapped here for the rest of the day. Nii Addy doesn't help by starting to cry.

'Foomo! Foomo!' Aunty Merley sees to him and the baby's tears wane as fast as they start. She turns to look at me and repeats, 'Foomo!'

Aunty Merley has the same resolve in her eyes I've seen today in both Dedei and Klu's eyes.

'Aunty M…' I begin.

'Who is your aunty? I'm your mamma d'you hear?'

I look down. This is serious. It always is when she wants to force the distinction between mother and aunty. I focus on the tribal mark on her cheek. Lots of people from Accra that are her age don't have tribal markings but I can imagine an infant Naa Merley opting into the disappearing tradition so that nobody she ever meets is going to know what a badass female she is.

The interesting scar moves a little when she gets especially animated or when she smiles like a kindly middle-aged lady.

She is a kindly middle-aged lady and she doesn't need a smile to overdo things. Smiling too much might get in the way of when she isn't kind to those who pose a threat to her and her family. She pushes a plate of food towards me which I haven't noticed before, expecting me to eat it. Aunty Merley is a kindly lady who can cook.

I exhale as quietly as I can. It takes longer than if I'd done it loudly. Klu comes and sits down next to me and the bowl of Palava stew his mum has made for me. So it's Klu and me, one side of the table, looking at the two Adjei women opposite. Aunty Merley stares back at me saying nothing.

Merley's the most seasoned criminal I've ever known. She has been ever since one Wednesday night when she took advantage of the two years I had left in the British childcare system.

She had told me, 'If my family isn't big enough the government will take away my house.'

I'd had foster carers before. Merley wasn't even the one I was with the longest. All of them had said nicer things than her, and made me do fewer chores, but none of them had been honest with me. She always was honest.

She's had nearly twenty years now of playing my mother, most of them with nothing in it for her. When I figure out her motive, I'll be a better criminal for it.

I sometimes think I am the only one who really knows how clever Aunty Merley is. As it is, she's mistaken for an ordinary, superstitious fifty-year-old African woman who goes to church regularly.

Aunty Merley leans back and shouts for the benefit of onlookers. I have to be interested now.

'Now!' Merley watches approvingly as I pull the bowl toward me.

She points, 'That park!'

Klu and I think it's an African rhetorical pointing.

'That park!' she repeats, still pointing. Klu and I look out of the window as directed at Shacklewell Park.

'They want to close that park. It's all here.' Aunty Merley produces a leaflet which she waves threateningly at us.

Klu is also apparently hearing about this for the first time, 'So?' he says, voicing my sentiments, 'There's another park down the road! A bigger park. A better park!'

'For you it's down the road. For little mammies that can watch their babies play over there from their windows, it's far!' She hits her palm against our table powerfully. 'No! They cannot close this one.'

'What am I supposed to do about it?'

'You grew up playing in that park and others like it in this borough.'

'Granted. But what am I supposed to do about it?'

'You have a friend that works for the council don't you? That girl with the big botoss?'

I remember the girl. She means Monica Asere.

'Yeah? A friend?' Dedei is enjoying herself.

My aunt pretends it isn't casual sex if she calls the women I've had it with my friends.

'Monica doesn't work for the council aunty. She is a lawyer who has represented the council in court…'

Aunty Merley interrupts, 'But it's all to do with the government. They're all the same.'

'No aunty, there are different departments, and none of my friends have got juice enough to stop anything like this! Parking tickets and planning permits maybe!' I look at the developer's leaflet. 'This has got the logo for the Greater London Authority on it.' The deadline for public consultation on the matter was last week according to the same leaflet.

'Chiaa!' Aunty Merley makes a spitting sound. 'There is nothing greater about these people.'

'Yeah but the deadline's passed for public...' I struggle, 'What I'm trying to say is this thing is being done from London City Hall, not Hackney Civic Centre.'

Aunty Merley huffs and puffs and blows my opinion down. 'If you let them, there'll be more crime!'

'More crime, because a park goes?' Klu contributes.

Although it's along the lines of what I'm thinking I scowl at him anyway. It would have been nice if they'd had this conversation before I had to be here. The leaflet has an unusually suspect business logo next to the crests of a bunch of east London boroughs. What looks like a hand cupped around a simple looking house. I remember it from somewhere. But where?

Aunty Merley answers her son. 'They don't understand that the more trees they cut down and the more grass they hide under cement, the more crime there'll be.'

'Yeah, maybe,' I sigh.

'Nii Nathan,' Aunty Merley explains patiently, 'nature reminds us we're part of something, the more trees they cut down the more like animals we become.'

She sits back thinking she's made her point and I let her think so. 'Nii Nathan! Don't let them do this, use any means necessary, like that man with the spectacles you and Klu had on your wall used to say.' Aunty Merley mimics Malcolm X and taps her index finger behind her ear. Her colourful headwrap tries it's best to detract from how black and white she's being in a grey world. 'Do you hear me? By any means necessary.'

She's probably got an AK-47 around here too.

Inner-City Eco Warriorism.

I walk out of the restaurant, hands in pockets, frowning at the offending park.

A Black boy of about eighteen years old tips his chin at me and puts his fist out for me to bump it. I think about putting my fist out to reciprocate before I realise I recognise the motorbike. He wears no helmet this time.

'Alright Nate?' he says using the familiar. I don't know his name but I know him from around. His voice doesn't carry any note of repentance at his part in this morning's thing with the tow truck and my car.

'Sup,' I say back to him.

I know as much about motorbikes as I know about women's dresses but I know enough to tell that this one is fast and I would be impressed if I knew what I was looking at. Superbike, nought to sixty in nought seconds type of job.

'Cromber wants to see you,' the rider says.

'Cromber wants to see me?' Why does everybody want to see me today? 'What for?'

Predictably the boy shrugs.

'When?'

'Right away! My man's been trying to call you for several minutes but you must have changed your number.'

'Tell Cromber... I don't do right away. I'll try and get over before the rush hour.

'Bruv. It's got to be now.'

'I'll be there.'

There's silence before the boy twists the handlebar and the motorbike's engine detonates into life.

'So, Klu's out?' he asks rhetorically, manoeuvring the front of the motorbike towards the road.

I stare at him. I don't care if he's asking off his own initiative or is sent to ask. I need him to know that just asking puts him in danger. Maybe no more danger than his life usually puts him in, but he was in danger now. He will only be safe if he leaves and never speaks to me like that again.

I don't watch him to see if he is moving off to a discreet distance. I don't care. There are ten other hoppers just like him who will see me not head to Cromber straightaway. I've told Klu he had nothing to fear from Cromber. This call to heel is a chance to get a guarantee and make sure all fifty of the people Cromber has rolling deep for him get word of that guarantee.

I hear Klu leaving, trying to say goodbye to his mother. Aunty Merley is not the kind of woman who accepts a farewell easily and she insists on arranging a return time before you go.

'These children, they see their elders and leave without saying hello or goodbye,' says Aunty Merley, one hand still gripping Klu as she watches the red motorbike disappear. 'And I think I know that boy and his mother... from somewhere...?'

'Maybe from church?' I suggest.

Aunty Merley nods at the possibility, then she asks, 'When are you going to save the park?'

'This afternoon.'

Aunty Merley's smile is so wide it's disconcerting before she bounces back into her restaurant.

'This afternoon?' Klu's look is perfect in it's scepticism. 'Who was that?' He juts his chin in the direction the hopper has gone.

'Nobody.'

I show him the pictures that were on my phone, and that Klu's son had taken such an interest in. Buki Nneka and the making of her new tattoo, 'Where do you go to get one as good as that?'

Klu gives me the answer I was expecting.

'Yeah.' I thought the same. 'Take me to Aldgate first though.'

'Yes sir Boss!' Klu shucks and jives.

After a short pause he asks, 'What's Dedei saying?'

I frown, 'Why didn't you ask her what she's saying?'

Klu explains, 'She's got a beef with me 'cau' I betrayed her friend.'

'Dedei and Leticia are friends?'

'Nawh mehn! But you know that Black woman sisterhood thing.'

'Didn't this new woman know about your BM?'

'Yeah! Exactly! She did.' Klu smiles at me. 'Dedei's pissed off with everyone really.'

A few seconds later Klu is still smiling at me.

'What?'

'We always thought… you and Dedei… you know?'

'What?' I say again but differently. I can see the grey car is two vehicles behind. The driver knows I'm in this orange urban monstrosity Klu drives.

'You know!' Klu's smile is temporarily replaced with a look of determination as he navigates a narrow road, 'Do the marriage thing!'

Before Klu can continue I interrupt, 'We're being followed. Flip a bitch.'

'Check! Flippin' a bitch!'

With most evasive manoeuvres you get a couple of seconds grace while people following you mistake somebody else's car for yours until they see the wrong number plate or a bald man in a turtleneck. The problem with driving a bright orange car is the driver of the grey car will know when he's not following us.

What Klu's car lacks in subtlety he makes up for in road craft and Klu loses the Hyundai faster than I managed to. 'If you can't beat them, confuse them!' Klu roars making sure we're alone then notes, 'Your car moves alright! But it ain't got that kick like my boy's got.'

As Klu's boy kicks I see an advertising hoarding again with the logo of the hand cupped around a simple looking house from the leaflet Aunty Merley gave me. This time I take my time and take notice of the name connected to the logo: 'Domain Management'.

After a couple more flips of saying nothing Klu asks, 'Who's after you? Black guy or white guy?

'What's the difference?' I ask.

Klu explains, 'White criminals kill you with no warning but for good reason. Black criminals kill you for no reason but you always see it coming. In fact, half the point of it is that the streets know it's coming and you still can't stop from getting it!'

Hoods don't stop – they just take a break...

Klu and I climb out of his car in a part of London that should really be ashamed of looking like it does, this close to the city district. We breathe in air that smells of old fruit and warm lamb.

Klu, ready for action, says, 'What have we got?'

'One guy, Hector Edmondson, loser. Burgled Buki Nneka. Might have done something to her. This is: find-out-what-he-knows-and-doesn't-know-he-knows.'

'Got you,' Klu salutes.

I lead the way to the address Lauriston sent me.

'Okay,' Klu braces himself. 'How we working it?'

I had been thinking about how to work this before the

Facebook revelation and Aunty Merley, but really this didn't need much thought, 'Today, we're gangsters!'

'Yessir!' The more fun Klu is having the more African he sounds and the more I worry.

'That do remind me!' Klu smacks me hard but cheerfully across my abdomen with the back of his open hand, 'You know it's kicking off! You know them two dead chicks?'

'Yeah?' I prompt Klu.

'Popo traced them to a house in Chelsea that they used to live in.'

I stop breathing but Klu doesn't notice or interrupt his story. So the two dead women lived in the house in the black and white photograph where Buki Nneka had lived before she had gone missing. The death threat on the iPod now has new meaning at least.

Klu says, 'People think Hackney is bad but they ain't taking into consideration Tower Hamlets man! Makes Newham look like, like... fuckin' Greenwich!'

Hector Edmondson lives on the fifteenth floor of a high-rise block of flats. There are two lifts, one serves the odd-numbered floors and the other serves the evens. One of the lifts is out of service and the other one smells of piss. It won't go to the floor we need but we step inside anyway.

Klu puts his hood up. 'I'll get off on the fourteenth and you get off on the sixteenth. In case he tries to run I come from below you come from above.' Klu pinches the air with his index finger and thumb, 'They call that a pincer movement.'

I look at him, sceptically, 'I don't think we'll be needing all that. This guy shoplifts and mugs old ladies!'

While Klu's in a rare careful mood I pass him a spare pair of bio-gel gloves. He turns his nose up at me and produces wool sports gloves. There's plenty of forensic to be left behind by those but they're standard issue Kappas. Suspects would be every thug with a violent previous.

The lift doors open with surprising enthusiasm on 14 and Klu steps out and points above nodding at me.

I sigh and shrug. Seconds later the doors perform the same act on 16 and I step out rubbing my gloves together. I take the stairs down to where Klu has already ascended his stairs.

'Clear?' I ask, not as sarcastically as all that.

Klu still serious, still looking around, nods.

I don't like the look of the letterbox flap so I rap the door hard with my right fist. I hope Hector Edmondson can feel the Black Power stance behind the knock and that he's appropriately moved.

Klu and I wait, ready.

'Who is it?'

'We're Nate and Klu to our friends,' Klu talks towards the letterbox, 'Mensah and Adjei to you!'

No reply. The pause makes me think there may be somebody else in there. This might be bad... but could be okay... I want to get away from here as soon as possible.

'We're looking for...' Klu looks up at me from where he talks through the letterbox.

'Mr Edmondson.' I say quietly.

Klu grimaces at me not hearing.

'Edmondson,' I say loud enough again so that even the man inside can hear me.

Klu nods and talking into the letterbox again says, 'We're looking for Edmond's son.'

'Okay... I see... to what is this... regarding?'

'We got some questions we got to ask him!' Klu answers.

'Well, he's not around right now. Can I give him a message?'

'Okay... we see,' I grin hoping I don't already like this guy too much to stop me getting the information I need. 'Can you step away from the door please?'

'Why?'

'Because we're about to kick it in and we don't want you to be hurt by accident before we can do it properly,' I explain.

Harassment – without violence
Maximum Penalty: 6 months imprisonment and/or a fine
Protection from Harassment Act 1997, section 2

We hear the man turn and run.

I nod at Klu, 'On one?'

Klu nods back and puts his hood down.

'Two… one!' We call as one, and as one we put a boot each to the centre of the door. The door bursts open with a minimum of fuss and considering the circumstances a minimum of noise.

Klu chases the retreating Edmondson.

I take a look around for anybody he may have been consulting with. A quick search shows there's nobody here but our man. This is fair enough and I am grateful to have found him home and not have to make messy enquiries about every crack or heroin house in the postcode.

When I reach the sitting room, I find Klu holding Edmondson over the edge of an open window. It shows a willing spirit because Klu doesn't know exactly what I want from the man yet.

Harassment – putting people in fear of violence
Maximum Penalty: 5 years imprisonment and/or a fine
Protection from Harassment Act 1997, section 4

Klu shouts. 'We know you did it! Bookey Knicker! We know you took her!

While Klu shouts, I breathe in the fresh air from outside.

'Alright Edmondson.' I quickly start from the beginning. 'The units at the community business centre at Stratford. You broke in. Stole some things and gave or sold them on.'

I ignore his stock denials to continue, 'What did you take? A set of keys? A purse?'

Edmondson shakes his head and with every it wasn't me and you've got the wrong man, I get more irritated and Klu forces him further out of the window.

'We know you did it. Maybe you went there more than once. Let's skip past all the denials, my friend's hands will get tired.'

'What did you take? Who did you see there?' Klu is out of breath faster than usual. The guy might be heavier than he looks. 'Who sent you?'

'What kind of police are you?' Edmondson asks shaking his head. I hold Klu back from pushing the man to his death right there.

'You can't kill me!' Edmondson screams. He now sounds more scared than he has been, as most of his weight transfers out of the window.

Klu isn't conceding Edmondson's point and he is offering to let gravity and concrete do the killing. He edges Edmondson further over the edge of the window singing, 'Ladies and gentleman and smackheads we have take-off! In case of a non-traditional landing please put your head between your thighs and kiss your arse goodbye!'

Threats to kill
Maxumum Penalty: 10 years imprisonment
Offences Against the Person Act 1861, section 16

I lend a hand securing Edmondson and add, 'I was just saying that on the way here!'.

'You was?' Klu says letting me help our junky.

'I was. I did.' I nod at Edmondson who has to crane his head forward to look at me. It's a funny angle we're hanging him at. 'In fact, I'm still saying it. We can't go around killing every white man that lies to us – I mean that's one job, or jihad if you will, with no end!'

Klu grunts, 'The longest journey starts with a single step my nigga!'

Edmondson moans. His eyes are coming into focus more. It's always interesting watching people coming off their highs. Not being in the business of taking or selling drugs I expect every user is different but I need Edmondson to sober up quickly and tell me whatever he knows.

Because he has to know something. Threatening to throw him out of a window by accident is a fucked-up state of affairs otherwise.

'Mister Adjei here thinks you don't care about dying but you said you can't kill me! See, that's how I know you're smart. You know we won't kill you. You're a fuck-up. I mean you also know that. No denying that. But you're still white.'

'He is that,' Klu grants.

'He is white isn't he?' I say, happy that he and I have found a shared belief.

Klu concurs again, 'Definitely white. Like a toilet bowl! One of them nice ones!'

'Your father probably doesn't like you but he'd take uhm… exception to a couple of Africans throwing you off the fifteenth floor in the wrong part of E2.'

'It's actually the sixteenth,' Klu points out, 'cos the ground floor is called ground floor innit but it ain't the ground yet.'

I nod, duly noting this point for future use, 'If we were to kill you it's important that we do it more quietly than throwing you from the sixteenth storey.'

'Same as for the funeral,' Klu grunts. 'Quiet like!'

'Amen! Or even if we were to kidnap you, we have to do it quietly! So your father can shake his head, send money for the ransom and other arrangements but not really give a fuck!'

'I've never broken into any place!'

Klu's disgusted with the junky, 'If that's your way of saving yourself you might as well kill yourself now!'

'The point is, I like a different approach. Let me show you a little trick.' With my thumb and forefinger I grab hold of Edmondson's lips.

'When I say *now*... my friend, cousin and brother here, will punch you in the throat and/or the chest. Hard enough to hurt but not hard enough to bruise. You will vomit because your toxicity is already fucked up. Then you can fall to your death. Everybody will say you were high and jumped or you had a bad reaction and fell. Alternatively you can tell us what we want to know and we can all go about the rest of our day.'

'Okay... I broke in but there was nothing worth anything... only papers!'

'Papers!' Two handed I bring the man back in closer to safety, 'What kind of papers?'

'Papers!' Edmondson wants to shrug

'Cash papers? Rizla papers? Handwritten? What kind of papers?'

'I dunno. Papers! Some of them were old and some were new with signatures and stamps.'

'Who sent you?'

He shakes his head.

'Who did you give them to?'

He shakes his head harder than before. This is an act of defiance beyond the polite lies he's been telling. I look him in the eye willing him to change his mind. He won't.

I say, 'Drop him.'

<u>Attempted murder</u>
Maximum Penalty: life imprisonment
Criminal Attempts Act 1981, section 4

The fit Edmondson throws calls our bluff. His body starts jerking in something akin to real life-ending seizures... but probably nothing an Edmondson can't fake.

We finally get him fully inside, let him go, and shivering he sinks to the floor.

'My brother!' he breathes out in relief! He tries to throw his arms around me but sags to the floor, unconscious.

'Nigga! He's not your brother!' Klu grins crouching next to the man. 'He's your anti-brother.'

Edmondson can't hear Klu's sage advice.

'He could be hours before he comes round!' Klu says, looking at me. 'You want to take him with us?'

I shake my head, taking off my gloves. Edmondson has nothing else for us and I guess we didn't like him all that much.

Inside two minutes, we're back at Klu's orange hatchback.

'That was some African gangster shit!' Klu takes off his gloves to search in his pocket for a car key. 'That thing with vomit in the throat, that is deep! Where'd you learn that?'

'I made it up, it's bullshit,' I say, taking my gloves off as well. 'You watched CSI New York lately? If you die violently, they can tell how many people you've shaken hands with that day and who's patted you on the back.'

Klu nods, 'And that's only what they want you to know

about the technology!'

'Did you notice anything about the flat?' I ask.

'It was a mess…'

'Yes,' I interrupt, 'but a clean mess.'

'Maybe he cleaned up before we came.'

'Junkies don't care about things like cleanliness. So Edmondson must have someone taking care of him.' What sounds like a cry in the distance interrupts me.

Klu and I look around. My eye travels to the window we hung Edmondson out of, but before it gets there I see a man falling towards us. Bystanders start screaming at the horrific sight they are witnessing. More people appear from nowhere.

Klu and I decide there is only one reasonable course of action. Normal, steady steps, no one sees us move towards his orange car, nobody watches us get in and drive away.

'Where to?' Klu asks, both of us looking in the wing mirrors at what is happening behind us, more than the road ahead.

I think about how this is as good a time as any to go and see Cromber. Then I think about the tattoo Buki recently got, and what papers she could possibly have had in that workshop of hers.

'You know what, drop me off at my lock-up… but first we're going to Vegas.'

'Vegas.' Klu points the car in the right direction. 'Cool!'

We're going to be up three hundy by Mare Street…

I look out of the window at Venturas and its strange mix of Los Angeles gang and Goth frontage. It is Hackney's most popular tattoo and piercing parlour but always looks quiet.

I've never had to fight anyone with face piercings. I fancy they act as handholds in brutal beatings.

'I don't think you're allowed to park here,' I point out, looking at the dark-red-painted zone following the course of the road.

'Fuck'em!' Klu spits.

<u>Bus Lane Violation</u>
Maximum Penalty: £80 fine increasing to £120 when unpaid within 14 days

'Sup Vegas!'

Vegas is a light-skinned Black man with a pierced tongue and lip. If he has eyebrows I can't see them.

He smooths his Mohawk hairdo. 'Nate plus Klu!' Vegas talking in heavy Bantu-accented pidgin English sends an uplifted fist for a bump with my associate Klu.

Klu looks at the fist blankly and I stay on the other side of the room so he can't try it with me.

'Err? Do you mind?' A large-sized Black woman is aggrieved by the added presence at her side. She's having a tiger paw tattooed on a breast and feels she's owed some privacy.

'Oh, we're the first niggas to see your left tit, yeah?' Klu says folding his arms and looking pointedly at her bared breast.

Vegas and Klu laugh and when they stop she is still kissing her teeth. She pulls her top up as much as she can.

I throw my phone to Klu and he calls up the pictures of Buki Nneka's new tattoo.

'Did you do this?' Klu shoves the phone in Vegas' face.

Vegas hmms and ahhs over the picture. 'Oh yer, course! See quality! See dertail… inking!'

'What phone number do you have for her?'

Vegas digs around in his pocket and no sooner has he got his phone out and unlocked it than Klu has taken it and under-armed it to me.

I quickly find the contacts directory and the name Bukey next to a picture taken right in this very room with Buki Nneka smiling warmly with Vegas.

I recognise the phone number as one of those I already have for her and that she hasn't been picking up all day.

'Is that it?'

Vegas nods, perplexed.

I throw his phone back to him. As I do Miss Tiger Paw isn't losing her attitude and shows she also has a keen eye, 'That's The Key!'

She adds, 'She's shit!'

This exclamation jolts me from my haze of low expectation and mulling over the day's incongruities. I haven't given any thought to whether Buki Nneka was any good at the singing thing but hearing the woman's work or persona summed up as shit affects me strangely. It takes a second to name the feeling. If I had to put a name to my emotion it's offended.

I look at the woman's face, my expression changing but looking back at me she knows it is time to shut up. I am feeling something negative towards her that I have no business feeling considering she has a breast out on show.

Something in my eye menaces or influences the behemoth of a woman into leaving.

Vegas talks to her wobbling bottom. 'Give us ten minutes! I go finish your distin...' he touches his own chest, 'sharp!'

'What else?' I breathe Vegas' way.

Vegas is jumpy around Klu anyway. Even more so than it's healthy to be. Vegas is the kind of man that owes money to people who try to send me after him. It's also the kind of job I refuse but recommend for Klu, but that's not the business we're here on today.

Vegas starts, 'Like two weeks now... the first time she came here...'

'Buki Nneka,' I interrupt, confirming the details as per her Facebook profile.

'Buki Nneka, she talk sey she get problem plus her man wey she scared and unhappy and all sorts of tings. Me – I no mind uhm because we all of us bore plus our spouse or?' Vegas tries to lull us into smiling with him. 'Then the second time she came...'

'Last week?' I affirm.

'Last week,' he re-affirms. 'Now she's talk say relationship finish-finish. How she think her husband not just be rich man but be rich criminal – brutal! So I told her to take it to some lawyers way I know um! Some very fine lawyers.'

Fielding didn't mention any lawyers – not even for that brief time he and Buki had gone their separate ways. Neither was any lawyer's address in his comprehensive file. 'You sent Buki Nneka to lawyers the week before she disappears.'

Vegas nods.

'She was here yesterday right?

'Yes, that was the last t...'

'What did the lawyers say?' I interrupt.

Vegas shakes his head violently, 'She said she didn't trust um! Her husband and her new boyfriend – she no trust um!'

'Which lawyers?' While I was inclined to ask about this new boyfriend Klu asks what are probably the most relevant question, 'Who were the lawyers?'

Vegas tuts himself, 'I forget his name self, his house dey for the area.' Vegas points south pre-empting local directions he's forgotten.

'Some big lawyer has just moved into our manor?' Klu affirms, incredulous. 'A lawyer that you got to scare off our girl and you forget his name.'

'Do you believe him?' I ask, a genuine threat of a question.

'No,' Klu answers simply.

'Why not?'

'Because I never believe him.' Klu flexes his neck and shoulder muscles and makes fists with his fingers.

'His offices are in Canary Wharf...' Vegas' memory starts returning, 'He gets one yellow babe for his hand-top... I got his contacts here somewhere.'

By yellow Vegas means Asian or a mixed-race woman. By hand-top he means the woman was with him or the lawyer has an Asian or mixed-race woman with him when he's tattooed or had the image tattooed somewhere between his wrist and his shoulder.

'It be her and him come and take one-one matching lovey-lovey tattoos for them both. Vegas scuttles over to a bleached-white skull that has its top sawn off cleanly. Inside are business cards and he ransacks it until he finds an item. He acts like it will make everything alright and pain-free this afternoon.

Concerned about proximity to Klu, Vegas hands me the card.

'What's this?' Klu makes shooting motions with his lips. 'Did she use proper lawyers or were they jokers?'

'Proper, it looks like.' I then read the words on the card: R. M. Laylor Solicitors.

If I was a detective this would be seen as a lead. Lawyers and trouble go hand in hand and so do lawyers and all kinds of papers. Edmondson took papers from Buki's former place of business and Edmondson is now dead.

'Her man, her new boyfriend. What did she say his name was? It was the boss of her record company. It'll be his office where she beshi there most of her days, that studio in Shoreditch...'

The confirmation that Fitz Beatz is Buki's boyfriend is all the information we require and it is time to hit the road.

Klu peels a fire engine red parking ticket from his windscreen and screws it into a ball before dropping it down a nearby drain.

'There's something hinky about your rich boy looking for this Bookey Knicker. She's a slag by all accounts.'

'We use a gun, she uses her body.'

'She would have fucked all the men in that reality house if the show hadn't got cancelled!'

Klu aimed his car towards my garage. 'You wanna go to Canary Wharf now or later?'

'Later. Drop me at my garage. Time to go and get my car.'

'Yessuh!'

'How did you know we'd be going to Canary Wharf?'

'Bruv, we're African. Juju innit!'

With a little help from Klu's loose interpretation of British driving laws in built-up areas we're soon close to where I keep my car.

Not missing a beat and changing in tone Klu looks at me, 'Throwing Edmondson out of that window. Do you think I did that?'

'No, and I am your alibi.'

'No, I don't mean physically obviously!'

I look at Klu, confused. Edmondson being thrown out of the window was as physical as it gets.

Klu explains, 'I wanted to throw him out the window and I made that joke about killing himself... then we were downstairs... then it's like he went out of the window. Maybe I have powers I don't know about.'

I shake my head at Klu. 'If you did you'd use it for good

like stopping kids from getting run over or getting that woman right here to give me a lap dance.'

Sea Air Land

I drive down the A12 at a comfortable overtaking speed of eighty miles an hour. The speed cameras decorating the dual carriageway have not been disabled but I want to get where I'm going fast.

Exceeding the speed limit
Maximum Penalty: 6 penalty points and a fine
Speeding, Road Traffic Regulations Act 1984, section 89

The traffic for the Blackwall Tunnel starts soon after the exit for Bow. I've never understood the fascination with south London. I take the West India Dock Road exit and drive over the painted arrows to CANNING TOWN.

On the last main road I pass groupings of Cromber's informal sentries. They're all virtual clones of the motorbike rider that has found me twice today. They stand looking in different directions as if they are the Neighbourhood Watch. Watching out for criminals and for cops...

This criminal stops between a three-storey building which has recently been renovated and turned into a nightclub and an old cinema that doubles as a church and a business conference centre. They are both nicer on the inside than the other buildings across town that Cromber owns. But that's because they're in a part of London that won't be fashionable for another ten to fifteen years, so they have to be. There's an improbably located shop next door wholesaling household goods. This random piece of property selling lamps, cabinets and suitcases is safely shut by the time the business of clubbing begins. All three of

Cromber's clubs come with small apartments that Cromber lives in from time to time as he plays a cat-and-mouse game with the police to frustrate the warrants for his arrest.

Three men in their early thirties sit on the bonnet of a luxury car, playing with their girls' hips. The girls in turn play with the car crests. These men are Cromber's lieutenants. Where their subordinates wear Evisu jeans and JD sports hoodies these guys wear John Smedley polo sweaters and platinum necklaces and rings. MTV cameras may turn up at any time. It is good to see some people having fun with this crime thing.

Their cars are parked illegally, daring their poor cousin traffic wardens to come and ticket the Bentley, the Acura or the Maserati.

They look at me like they're not expecting me. So the lookouts I've passed and possibly the ones on the main roof haven't beeped them to say I am on my way?

'Gents,' I hail them.

'An Audi bludh?' they sneer, looking at my car.

I shrug submissively, and my eyes like dipped headlights ask, 'Where is he?'

They're not ready to let me move around them and their discussions about me and the car I'm driving.

'His BMW was waste enough – now man's in an Audi y'knaa!' one says.

'This nigga's not serious!' agrees the other.

The men peel away and stand in front of me blocking my entrance to the club that Cromber's office is in this month. Their young females, who in their sex-and-the-city shoes, may actually be beautiful under all the make-up, ignore me. It is a shame, for idiots they have good taste in women. Two of the men are the exact same height as me and the third is only slightly shorter, with his arm in a sling.

I look at Mossi carefully. I had hoped to avoid him and his accusing eyes that bore into me, but he and his friends' man-wall have made our second confrontation necessary.

We stand in peace facing each other waiting for one of us to make a move.

Above, there's the sound of a finger with an overgrown nail tapping on a window.

Cromber's in the club. I don't look up to the office but look at the lieutenants so I can enjoy watching them part reluctantly.

The last to move is Mossi, still senior to the others in terms of length of time spent outside prison. He leans in towards me, trying to make me take a step back.

I don't. There's another rap at the window and I burst into a wider smile.

'I don't like you,' says Mossi.

The others fall silent and I wonder if this is known as a death threat in their circle.

Mossi's threat doesn't concern me as I know as a matter of instinct that Mossi can never be the end of me. I make my way through a series of doors marked Staff Only. None of the lieutenants are providing me with an escort so either Cromber is running a clean joint here or they're hoping I steal something to give them an excuse to kill me. I arrive at a room from where I hear loud music.

I knock on the door that feels to my internal compass like the room that the tapping came from.

'Yuh,' a voice says, 'enter!'

I enter.

When I walk in Cromber doesn't look up. His fingers hovering over the keyboard tell me he's probably playing Tetris.

It occurs to me that Mossi hasn't even told Cromber I'm the cause of his new sling. In any case ignorance or Cromber serve as my dual protection.

Cromber, with eyes that look like they're trying to pop out of his face, is an unusual kind of gangster for the east London scene. It's like he should be shooting children in a mine somewhere, but he's here. And he's on the television screen he's watching.

He wears a double-breasted American-style gold suit with five buttons down the front identical to the one the evangelist preacher on the television is wearing. The brother on the screen's permanently open mouth and heavy gestures don't seem incompatible with the pagan lyrics from the full blast Nigerian hip-hop song playing.

UK based negroes and negresses didn't used to show such American levels of emotion until the late nineties. The church scene puts me in mind of how Cromber was set up in business by the state. He used to own worthless tracts of land in Hackney Wick which he sold for exorbitant amounts of money to the government for venues for the Olympics.

I nod my head slightly to the music and think of the girls outside.

I imagine Cromber is keeping me waiting to show he's the one with power here.

I don't sit down so that Cromber can't say he didn't offer me a seat and expect me to get up, which he knows I won't and it will be a massive diss and people will start bleeding. And all because I'd sat down when I wasn't tired. I won't even sit down now if he invites me – just to strike my own blow for equality between the unequals. I keep myself busy picking lint off my shoulders.

On the off-chance he can come up with something, I have left the iPod from the Chelsea house with Lauriston. For all the difference it would make I also told him where I was headed.

Best case scenario he's able to undo whatever voice distortion programme has been used by the person who recorded the death threat. Worse case scenario, Lauriston doesn't deliver but at least the property stolen from a house where a policeman was assaulted this morning isn't found at my home.

There are masks, a holograph-style poster of the Last Supper and a banner on Cromber's wall with a host of African sayings on it. It's the sort of thing hanging in Aunty Merley's café and her home but she has a lot of humanity. Cromber doesn't. I don't remember seeing all the Africana here before.

In amongst the usual wisdom about not chasing a madman who steals your clothes whilst you're bathing, empty barrels and long journeys with monkeys, one in particular gets my attention:

'It is because of beauty that a woman holds her breasts when she runs not because she fears they will fall off.' – Fefe ne efe

'It's from Ghana.' Cromber says to me.

That's when I realise I'm smiling. I stop.

It's like Equatorial Africa on our side of the building!

'You're from Ghana, right?' Cromber asks in his best Lagos-Los Angeles accent.

'Something like that.' And after that I allow a further, 'My mother was.'

'You like all this, innit?' Cromber begins with showing off, 'I have three clubs, y'knaa!'

'I know,' I nod.

'They are always trying to shut me down... sometimes they do,' Cromber reflects. 'Then I move to the next one, buy back the last one they closed... complicated, big stuff!'

'I know,' I nod.

He means he's greedy. Cromber makes more money on a Sunday with the churches than most people make in a year but he still runs one of the largest cocaine distribution networks in London. Sometimes he buys from Fanny to supplement his inventory and sometimes whatever cursed Africans can carry in their stomachs is enough. He also has something complicated going with scamming white people that don't believe in the Bible but who are gullible when photos of women from Brazil are emailed to them.

'What were my boys saying to you?' Cromber sneers...

It's very rude of him to tell me things I already know and demand in exchange an answer to a question he should already know the answer to. I say, 'That they don't like me.'

Cromber beats out a little drumbeat on his fat stomach. 'The usual, ehh? Yeah, they don't like you. Neither do I, I don't like anybody! But I respect you. That's why I ain't sent them to give you this message the old-fashioned way.'

Hoppers had tried to christen their crew The Cunning Town Boys hoping it would take but so far we and everybody else just called them The Nigerians or Cromber's People.

They aren't cunning. Cromber has tried to get me to work for him before and I never have. I should be grateful Cromber is not one of those roll-with-us or get-rolled-over type gangsters. He is satisfied to leave me to my own devices as long as I don't get in his way.

'I'm gonna need you to back off your little search.'

'What?'

'Buki Nneka. That omoge, The Key.'

I keep my eyes on his so they don't dart around my sockets scrolling through my day trying to establish something that explains Cromber's request.

'What?'

'You're looking for her. I need you to stop. Cease, desist and all them words there…'

'What makes you think I'm…'

'Ay! Who the fuck knows why you're doing what you do when you're doing it, yo! You know and I know that you can be a real Name-your-target-after-the-arrow-has-landed-type dude.'

'Even if I am, what's it got to do with you, who I'm looking for or not?'

After a pause Cromber looks at me then he emits an hmm, shakes his head and hmms a couple more times.

Somewhere between the hmms, it comes. Fielding's briefing on Buki Nneka's past.

He had said that most of her Black African friends were my kind. And that new Black African slavers who helped her come here were pursuing her for money he claimed she still owed.

Here, this side of the tracks that are the Docklands Light Railway or cocaine footprints, reside exactly the kind of men a Buki Nneka knew would keep coming back for more while there was more to get. If Fielding had been telling the truth…

Cromber and I watch each other's eyes for answers.

Cromber invades the silence, 'You don't drive cars like me, all them cars outside are mine y'know. How much money you got on you right now? It'll be one jib as usual right? Working capital.'

'Yeah,' I agree. 'Less some bribe money to a schoolgirl.'

'One thousand pounds!' Cromber's Black face is all contempt. His facial expressions are thick like he has more layers of skin than average. When he sweats, faint streaks of powdered salt cover his face.

Cromber's interest in Buki Nneka adds to the list of possible suspects. He continues, 'You been working with the Turkish wholesalers? Ten years now? More? You should be seeing the fruits of your unrighteousness by now. What, five thousand a week? Ten thousand at Christmas? Chicken feed!'

When gangsters get excitable like this I can get shot any time so I might as well make sure I don't go out on my knees but I say nothing still opting to listen.

'You know what makes me laugh about you Ghanaians?'

And Cromber is happy to be listened to.

'You guys work so hard and never have anything to show for it. Feed your family Lidl scraps, send money back to Challeyland, give the rest to us pastors then you die eating nothing but cornflakes! Drugs is where the money's being paid now and if you weren't such a small-time Challey you'd know about that.'

I look at the window while listening to Cromber.

'You know how many of your big-bum women we get in here with their noses open? Yeah they've got Jesus and He saves but they also need a nigga that spends!' Cromber reminds me of Dedei and Tony and how the whole Klu grudge got started.

'When we steal, we steal properly and when a Nigerian kills you know you're dead yeah! They say Ghana's the gateway to Africa but Nigeria is the destination muthafucka!' Cromber laughs now. He leans his head back with both hands across his stomach and laughs and laughs. He concludes with, 'When I've finished robbing these guys... I'll go back to Lagos... open another church.' He looks at me and can tell I'm unmoved but I'm taking in his words. 'No more Buki Nneka for you, right?'

Is he offering me a job with his exhortations, is he warning me against entering his game or is this all about Buki but trying to make it seem like it isn't? I'd like answers but I probably won't get any here now, not from Cromber.

It annoys me that this culture-confused prisoner in waiting thinks he can order me around and it annoys me even more that I'm about to leave here with him thinking that he has.

So it's my turn to talk.

'You know what I don't understand about you Nigerian gangsters. You were way ahead on information crimes. The system had to create laws for you. Yardies used to rate you. You guys used to make more than them without touching a Class A – C and you ran back to Lagos… nothing owned under your real names. Now your boys are out here with the same old guns and territory bullshit. Why did you fall back on the drugs and…?' I'm tempted to throw in human-trafficking to see if that is how he knows Buki Nneka but decide not to.

Cromber enjoys the question and the answering of it. The pause is only for him to decide if he's going to answer simple, or use visual aids.

'A lot of hard work, fam! One taker from ten thousand emails. With this other stuff, today I have it – tomorrow I sell for big money! Besides, they're creating new laws and creating new jail sentences. They're bringing out these old women who've sold the medals their husbands won in Germany. Juries are sending us down hard for that shit, so it's not worth it. It's a shame…' Cromber leans back in his seat. I can't tell for sure with his sunken eyes but he looks the way he did just after he had finished laughing a while ago. 'But we still cover all the bases. Muthafuckaz who think there's any princesses left to rescue deserve to get their shit took! – Ahlie?'

'You don't,' I submit.

'With the A – C stuff you're fucking with bank money. You

can't fuck with banks! They send people that don't get tired. Drugs is just… fucking with people. Nobody cares about people really.' Cromber rests his hands across the muscle and fat.

It's with this posture that emphasises his abdomen that I realise how out of place Cromber is in this newly redesigned office of his. I see Buki Nneka's hand in designing a beautiful space at odds with its inhabitant.

'And you got to make as much money from this narcotic business as possible. You know they're gonna legalise these drugs soon right?'

'I hear things like that,' I nod, noting he's not threatening my life now but I wonder how long before he does when he finds out I'm still looking for Buki.

'When it goes legal, when it's the same as coffee or orange juice, the only people to make money from this shit is gonna be the white people. I've already got my next move worked out. Well, you'll find out about that when you find out.'

Cromber stands, ending this, 'Me and you are fully clear on laying off Buki Nneka?'

'We're clear.'

'Good. You're a smart nigga! Always was.'

I've almost reached the door when Cromber adds, 'I'm hearing you're with this Shampoo Crew?'

I think about my answer, and because I want to leave a mystery of my own behind, I'm cryptic, 'That would be telling.'

Don't think you're big just cos you go to the gym!

Back on the ground floor of the club I make my way to the exit.

I haven't discounted what Fielding said about African

gangsters chasing Buki for money after getting her into the country, but I haven't accepted it either. Cromber isn't involved in coyote immigration stuff that I know of but if there was some truth to it, perhaps it could lead to finding Buki Nneka after all. Also I know where to find Cromber just as easily as he knows where to find me... but I move faster.

'What did you two have to talk about?'

I believe it's Mossi's voice and I can only make out the silhouette of a powerfully built man, which also matches Mossi, sitting at a VIP booth of the deserted club. All the lights of the club have been switched off save the bulbs above the bar. This is Mossi's problem right here. Over-compensation. Real men with power have been content to meet me in their natural environment. Mossi here feels the need to manipulate his surroundings to appear frightening. As my eyes get used to the dark I can see the whole thing has been staged, and not just to make up for already being one knock-down behind today.

The girlfriends are not even around to serve as a diversion. Instead there's the turn-off that is Mossi's v-neck dipping to show his muscled chest. Even with his arm in a sling he looks bigger than he did this morning. Still, I figure for every pound he gains in the gym, he loses more of his edge from having a small army to do his fighting for him. I can take him, and beating him up would be worth the effort as it had been with Tony.

Maybe this is a different kind of set-up to this morning. Maybe the girl with the lips has a gun or he has all his boys waiting outside to use the personal defence of their friend Mossi as a pretext for killing me when Cromber or the police ask.

Cromber is essentially another criminal having fun. Mossi is a different proposition. He needs everyone reacting to him with respect. Respect he might gain some day, but not today.

After pitying Mossi's attempt to look sinister I forget what his question was but remember I will not be answering any more questions here anyway.

'I really don't like you,' the figure in the corner says before taking a sip from what is probably an expensive glass of wine.

I lean back on the bar and toe the bar stool. It's heavier than it looks. I wouldn't be able to swing it fast enough unless I lost my temper and then I might miss.

Mossi has never liked me. Before the broken arm Mossi didn't like me, and even before the Klu-and-Tony thing he didn't like me. We have known each other ever since we were juvenile delinquents. Even before I met him I had heard of another African around my age in the post room of another crime organisation across town. Then we started driving and we met. Mossi was far bigger than he is now and I was leaner. Back then Mossi didn't like me because you couldn't like other boys in our business. Other boys can get you robbed, prosecuted or killed.

Before we could get to that Mossi had become a strung-out cocaine addict and he wasn't a rising gang-star any more. Mossi had stopped going to the gym and lost weight and status. Somewhere in the midst of his year and a half's ignominy I gave him money to keep him from living on the streets.

When Mossi came back under the wing of the Nigerian pastor with hundreds of thousands of pounds to invest in his London underworld sideline, he hadn't repaid me at all, let alone shown any gratitude. Instead he resented me as one of the people from the old days who saw him when he was down. Then Klu beat up his friend Tony before I 'deported' Tony and stole their guns.

I broke Mossi's arm in front of these new people from these

new days.

I didn't mention the guns to Cromber who may or may not be in cahoots with Mossi in this little sideline. My exemplary silence means Mossi is at my mercy again, because I follow a street code. Again I'm better than Mossi because those same complicated sets of principles dictate Mossi should exact justice, or get the guns back.

Even if I had asked Mossi for my money back we'd still be here. Him not as big as he used to be, and me bigger than I was. I hope that this episode too will pass as a normal gangster misunderstanding and we go back to standard antagonism amongst professionals but Mossi holds grudges.

'Cromber might have forgotten but I haven't,' Mossi states.

'Cromber never mentioned the guns. I wonder why that is?' I say mocking Mossi with the question but not the tone… My eyes are almost fully accustomed to the dark now. Cromber also didn't mention my fight this morning with Mossi.

'Cromber won't be in charge forever bro!' Mossi says in a way designed to have me ask what that is supposed to mean, then he sneers, 'D'you know that Cromber wanted to hire you to find out who'd taken our guns… but seeing as Tony disappeared too, we didn't need no Black Banacek in the end. Cromber won't believe Tony didn't take the guns. He would have come after you by now. I believe Tony. I'm only looking at you now wondering if you did what you did to him, to take the guns or cos he hit that lil' bitch sister of Klu's… Deedee.'

I say nothing. It all sounds like a lazy bluff but I say nothing.

'Tony ain't got no friends in Malawi y'knaa. They've all been firingsquad'd or fled. Tony didn't have long to live. Them are some United-Nations-type warrants you got waiting for him at every airport, port…'

'Malawi is landlocked. There are no ports.' I smile at him.

'Are we done here?'

He looks at me... smiling at him. He should be thinking I'm smiling like a man that likes his fights unstaged, or I'm looking like a coward.

I don't like overestimating my foe. It's just as counter-productive as underestimating them, and it usually costs more in time I don't have, making preparations for capabilities my opponent doesn't have.

'Yeah! Yeah man, that's all for now.' Mossi sips from his wine glass.

It is as I approach my car that a question poses itself in my mind and stops me in my tracks.

What if the guns I stole really were Cromber's? That would raise some interesting questions about what Cromber and Mossi were going to do with so many of them.

Leveraged Hustle.

Klu and I stand outside the office of R. M. Laylor Solicitors. I take a look around. The connecting tube station and elevated light-railway stations make this a terrorist target covered by dozens of remote controlled CCTV lenses with invisible motion-detecting lasers. Breaking into a complex like this is damn near impossible unless the plan involves finding a shop or office to hide in until the evening. I don't have time for that and can't bring Lauriston with me to hack into their security systems and the lawyer's records.

Klu follows me over to a phone box. I lift up the phone receiver and press buttons and am happy to hear beeps and tones audible over the sound levels of this commercial district.

'Stay here and when I give you the nod, hood up.' Klu kisses his teeth at me. His hood is already up now and for me to suggest he wasn't going to keep it up in circumstances like this is insulting but he lets me finish, 'Go in and get whatever they're shredding, then man this phone.'

One hand in my trouser pocket I dial the number for R. M. Laylor Solicitors.

'This is an urgent message for a Mr Laylor about his car. It's being towed.'

Less than a minute later and on cue a man in an expensive double-breasted suit runs out of the front of the office and into me.

'Ouch,' I say putting a hand to his breast pocket as if to ward him off bumping into me again.

'Sorry…'

'That's okay,' I say, putting my other hand against his side, 'Don't worry about it!'

He's distracted and nods politely at me before he heads off to check on his car. I watch him go, then examine the two phones I've just stolen from him. The phones only count as two of the four things I've lifted off him but they are definitely the most useful. I check the recently dialled lists of the most expensive phone and the only familiar name there is work attached to the same landline I phoned just over a minute ago.

I hit redial and a woman's voice replies quickly.

'Hello Mr Laylor!'

This is good. It means the office my victim has just left has caller ID so I must be Mr Laylor however different I sound.

'Hello,' I say, coughing. 'Who's speaking?'

'Roxanne!'

She's offended. She has either been working for Mr Laylor for a long time or they've slept together.

'Sorry Roxanne, I didn't recognise your voice.' I continue coughing to disguise my voice. 'I need you to shred all case files and whatever we have for Buki Nneka.'

'Sir?' Roxanne sounds further confused. 'But don't we have a duty to notify?'

'Yes, do that but not from the office phone…'

'What's going on?'

I carry on, coughing and whispering and obscuring the mouthpiece of the phone, 'We'll keep the computer records but everything on paper has to be destroyed now, d'you understand? And do not use the office phone for anything pertaining to this.' I end the phone call shouting, 'My car!' to make sure Roxanne doesn't dare ring back.

I give Klu the nod and keep checking the way Laylor went to make sure he doesn't come back to the office to inconvenience our operation. I'm looking forward to reading the files they have on Buki Nneka. The case itself and reading between the lines will produce a treasure trove of information about where to go from here.

Suddenly I remember I haven't polished my shoes like I should since leaving Hector Edmondson's flat. I take a seat in front of a shoeshine man on a bench that looks very artistic and intentionally uncomfortable to deter all but the most fatigued of shoppers and businessmen with the dirtiest shoes.

As the shoeshine man gets to work on my shoes I check contact names in both Laylor's phones under B and N for Buki Nneka, G and F for Grayson Fielding, and P and F for Patrick Fitz. No matching names or names interesting enough to be aliases with the same initials.

I go to my third of four stolen items. I took the wallet out of sheer habit. I'm surprised to find £500 in crisp fifty and twenty pound notes. Nothing like a lawyer of questionable ethics to appreciate the untraceability of the average ATM withdrawal. I clip the monkey to my £980 roll. Apart from the notes, the wallet holds the standard condom, gold bank and credit cards including American Express, but no receipts or pictures. I'll bin it later.

I've never made a habit of picking pockets. Londoners are too keen on their personal space for it to work but Laylor had been distracted, fretting over what was probably a fine number with a set of the finest alloys.

I took the keys just to piss him off, I'll dump the car remote in case it has satellite tracing but keep the house and office keys which might come in useful later.

To my surprise and the shoeshine man's shin, Klu throws a pen drive at me and turns to leave all in one seamless motion like he's performing a subtle funky house-dance step. In silence, I immediately plug the pen drive into my smart phone.

The man shining my shoes leans back, finished. I give him double his listed price, 'I'll have another one please, mate. I've been in some dirty places today.'

The bemused man shrugs and reaches for more polish.

My phone uploads information from the pen drive that has R. M. Laylor Solicitors physically printed on it and whose contents are labelled Buki Nneka, plus miscellaneous letters that make less sense than the letters after Laylor's name on his business card.

As well as some generic legal service information bumf I see a prominent folder called Domain Management. I click on it. That house-in-a-hand logo again, shipping schedules, dockets, invoices. If I have time I will look into Domain Management later.

The uploading of the pen drive's contents continues satis-factorily as a young woman I take to be Roxanne steps out of the office of R. M. Laylor Solicitors. The girl, being as pretty as she is, explains why Klu was in and out so quickly. Pretty girls are very easy to intimidate because they're already frightened when their beauty doesn't have the effect on a person it's been having on others since they've been thirteen years old, let alone when the shouting starts.

Roxanne hesitates outside her workplace. She can go to the police and tell them about the stolen files she was recently asked to destroy for disreputable reasons. Or she can call their client.

If Roxanne rings any of the numbers I have for Buki then they're trying to warn her and the lawyers are clean. If Roxanne rings anybody, a) whose surname isn't Nneka, b) any of today's players, c) anybody who also shouldn't know about Buki's private business, then the lawyers are dirty, which my instincts tell me they are.

My hoped for option is that Roxanne rings a number for Buki that I don't have, so I will have found her. Then I won't phone the lawyer to tell him where to find his valuables because I will be too busy drawing a line under this whole day.

Looking at something she has written on her hand I see Roxanne begin to dial. The operation really is going well beyond my wildest expectations.

'*Noko*!' Frowning, Klu nods at me making sure I'm ready.

Noko means nothing. There is no word for zero in the language, so the word for nothing does the job instead.

'*Pawoh*,' he says next.

Then he adds a '*Nehu*'.

'Zero. Seven. Nine... Klu is reciting the numbers Roxanne is dialling at me in Gā, loudly so a distracted Roxanne ignores him as just another excitable African talking loudly on his phone. Aunty Merley taught Klu the words for numbers in Gā, and Klu taught me. This has come in useful over the years.

'*Enumo shi ete*,' I hear him say next.

Five then three.

But the *shi* in between the two words. Does Klu mean five then a three or five repeated three times?

When Roxanne finishes dialling and Klu finishes reciting, I work out that five three times gives a phone number which makes sense. I see Roxanne talking into the phone briefly.

I take my phone and dial the number. According to the call log it has been dialled a lot recently in the cheaper of Laylor's two phones but has no name attached to it.

I swear as I hear half a ring at the other side.

I redial:

'The number you're calling cannot accept any calls right now. Please try again later.'

Blank. This is the message I and apparently Grayson Fielding are getting for all of Buki's numbers. Would Buki have discarded the phone that quickly or is it someone else that Roxanne called and warned? I'm hoping this doesn't involve going on another search especially if the people on the other side ditch the number and any others they have in the lawyer's dialled list or in the shredded correspondence.

I rise from my double deluxe shoeshining session and I decide that I will try again later, when I receive a text message. It's from Fanny:

'THAT'S FINE. ONE HOUR AT THE CUT.'

That's strange, Fanny has sent me a text message by accident. I change numbers a lot and to many of my contacts I'm nothing more than eleven digits in their call logs and every so often my eleven digits get mixed up with someone else's. It's strange because I don't remember Fanny making this sort of mistake before and because it is the kind of message he would send me. It's highly improbable he has another associate like me. But I'm too busy right now to be anything more than mildly curious.

'Nathan Mensah!' A voice calls out.

I see two white men looking and pointing at Klu. Only one of them has a police uniform on but Klu takes off running anyway without confirming what the second man is about, or which of them is doing the shouting.

'Stop! Police!'

Of course Klu doesn't stop.

From my place at the shoeshiner's I watch as these two men scramble down the upward escalator, bounding down three-four steps at a time and chasing after Klu. It's Klu they're chasing but they think it's Nathan Mensah.

Why? Klu wouldn't have used my name as an alias under any circumstances. I was expected here today, but why? The answer to that can wait.

Klu drops the bag of shredded papers he is carrying in my hands as he runs past.

I head south towards London Bridge.

'Fuck!' Somebody grabs my wrist.

Klu has crossed the bridge to my eastern side and turned his jacket inside out so it is now bright red and black instead of green and black. There are plenty of IC3 males wearing dark suits. Klu takes a look at the time on my watch face. 'They'll tow my shit!' he's thinking about his car and the eight minutes he has remaining on the metre. 'What did the cops want?'

I shrug. 'I didn't have time to ask!'

It all could just have been about the lawyer reporting having his pocket picked. I see a woman in a Burberry jacket at the other end of London Bridge. I make to follow her, just for a direction to walk in.

I walk making sure Klu's monitoring my change in direction. I see him already mid-nod and look quickly back to the woman.

A police car headed north over the river suddenly switches on its siren and lights. It doesn't stop by either of us and neither of the two officers it carries look my way or Klu's.

'That'll be the police dodging the traffic to get home early,' Klu says. 'Fuck!' he repeats, 'Is it the dude and the window?'

It's the banner I now see before me with the logo I've been seeing on and off all day and those words I'd more recently learnt to recognise: Domain Management. The green digitalised fingers encircling the orange house.

I put my hands on it, and they somehow make it real.

That and the, 'What the fuck are you doing?' question Klu has for me.

My hand goes from the screen-printed palm to the house. Now I see it's amber not orange.

'Klu.' My left hand returns to my side while my right massages my forehead above closed eyes. 'What would you say if that thing with your mum's park has something to do with this woman I'm looking for?'

How much for just the borough?

'Anything's possible in London town baby!' Klu says. 'But how are you working that out?'

'I'm not sure yet.' I answer him truthfully.

Behind us a police car or possibly a motorbike emits a familiar siren sound. It might be an abuse of power, drills, or actual police work widening the net looking for me. The problem with being guilty of the wide array of crimes that I have committed today and the kind Klu's always committing is that I cannot be sure who the police are looking for or how hard they're looking.

As we enter City Hall we are approached by a security man.

'We're here for a community-interest group…'

'The regeneration meeting?' asks the security man being unusually helpful.

Within a minute a regeneration meeting has me sat watching it from an observers' gallery high above a big boardroom table with thirty seats around it. I look at a set of very excited looking bureaucrats who all seem too enthusiastic about a meeting taking place at home time on a Thursday afternoon. Klu has got himself a cup of tea. He stirs the tea with a plastic stirrer and comes to join me.

'When are we getting out of here?' Klu asks. It might only be in my imagination that a few heads incline upward at us, but it's enough so that Klu has my attention over the custom branded R. M. Laylor Solicitors 32 MB pen drive.

I close what little personal space is between my play-cousin and I and press a finger to my lips then pinch my earlobe with my other hand before pointing to the forum downstairs.

After a few minutes of community-type chit-chat we hear a phrase that actually pricks Klu's attention: '…the five borough area.'

'That sounds like that tri-borough thing in New York.'

'But this is London,' I whisper back in Klu's own abrupt fashion provoking him to develop his line of thinking.

'Five borough area. Where's that then?'

'Hackney is in the five-borough area with Newham, Tower Hamlets, Waltham Forest… and Greenwich I think. In the aftermath of the Olympic Games the Mayor wants Hackney and the other boroughs to merge and have the same ratio of rich and poor people. London's thirty-two boroughs will be reduced to six.'

Klu starts ranting about how uniting the boroughs was another step towards a world he didn't like the sound of, and I interrupted him with more immediate concerns, 'Pay attention Klu! The point is when you hear about any kind of development in the five-borough area prick up your ears. Cos they're talking about us. This is it. They're talking about your mum's park right here. Right... here!'

'All of this for Shacklewell Park?' Klu looks at the big boardroom table and the important-looking people around it and the oversized projector screen.

I scan the scene down there fully, with my phone. I zoom in on the only empty seat at the table. There in front of the empty chair is a familiar name on the Domain Management name badge.

Most of the speakers remind the other participants who they are as they start talking but I don't care now about them because Grayson Fielding is supposed to be here now but he isn't. He would have been easily the most interesting man here. The only other person of interest is the Deputy Mayor, Bradley Chalk. He doesn't look happy to be here. He looks downright put upon in fact. I can tell because he slides down into his seat and his eyes wonder up. He sees me, tenses, looks more intently at me, sits up and pays a special attention to the papers in front of him that had just been missing a moment ago.

This is where my interest in Bradley Chalk begins. Each time he looks up at me, images of the man at my apartment block are projected into my head with more intensity.

The meeting's speakers merge into one with their statistics and pie charts so that I can't connect them to my Shacklewell Park grievance. The whole thing flies over my head. There is no other business.

As the grey suits at the meeting stream out of the room they are replaced by colourfully-dressed Ghanaian cleaners. I nod at the Deputy Mayor trying to signal to him that I will be seeing him soon.

Klu and I step into a lift followed by a woman dressed like Letitia had been this morning. Ignoring us she faces the front for two floors before she senses Klu's eyes boring into her body. Klu makes a triangle shape with the opening space between his thumbs and forefingers, and the woman looks back to see him looking earnestly at his hands with his palms pressed together prayer style. She turns back facing the direction of the doors. Klu rubs those same hands together and licks his lips. As the lift rises so do my hopes that Bradley Chalk is who I am hoping he will be.

Klu and I need to remain at City Hall for a while longer until the heat from the police outside and the other end of the bridge reduces. The woman dressed like Letitia gets out at the seventh floor followed by Klu, who smiles at me as he says, 'See you later, bruv.'

I continue on to the top floor. I take in the dirty looks from two Black women in the reception area in front of the lift before they approach me full of hostile suspicion that makes me feel at home. There's a third desk and chair, empty in the reception area.

Both women now smile at me, a visiting Black man and bat their eyelids in welcome. I give them a wide smile back and add a wink that even baby Nii Addy hadn't managed to get from me. I point at the door which has Bradley Chalk's name on it.

'Please cancel anything the Deputy Mayor has scheduled for the next half an hour,' I say smiling, before I enter into the big office not waiting for a reply and lock the door behind me.

'You know who I am?' I ask the man inside the office and put my hand out for him to shake, 'My name's Nathan Mensah. We are neighbours, Mr Deputy Mayor.'

I look around the office and soon find what I am looking for – a tray of loose pen drives labelled Mayor of London. I hope by now the Deputy Mayor recognises me as the man he saw this morning while he was at his girlfriend's place, the one with the sexy name and broken-into car.

'Where is the Mayor?'

'He's in New York at a conference,' he says, adding, 'Why do you want to see me?'

'Just a social visit from a concerned London resident.' I grin showing too many teeth like a wolf.

'Is this blackmail?' He asks me.

'No,' I answer like it's a matter of fact. 'Do I look like a blackmailer?'

First Grayson Fielding treats me like a private detective and now the man that may be on his payroll takes me for a blackmailer.

'I read somewhere that you were a successful businessman before you became Deputy Mayor?'

'Yes, I made money.'

'That's good. And now you've got a family – a nice wife and two lovely children. All that positive stuff the media loves.'

Bradley Chalk looks anxious but tries to relax.

'You have any bugs in here?' I ask Bradley Chalk.

He hesitates.

'Recording devices?' I clarify, before suggesting, 'Let's go out to the balcony, just to be sure.'

From his body language the Deputy Mayor was in two minds whether to come out onto the balcony. I get up anyway and head for the sliding door to the balcony. Bradley Chalk joins me.

A strong wind blows from west to east. At this altitude the wind feels more personal than it does at ground level. On the ground it feels like the wind is going about its business. I put the collar of my jacket up and watch the River Thames. The green-brown water looks the same from up here.

Not saying anything to him yet I check to make sure the R. M. Laylor Solicitors' file is being downloaded into the blank municipal pen drive I took from inside.

'Mr Deputy Mayor, I'm going to tell you the truth.'

He frowns while I continue.

'I've spent the day lying and being lied to because of... the business I'm involved in, while you've spent the day lying and being lied to because you're a politician. I also take it that your wife and the media don't know you've got a girlfriend hidden away in a posh apartment in Hackney.'

The Deputy Mayor makes no comment.

'So, let's give ourselves a break from all the lying and subterfuge. What I need from you first of all is to prevent any development that involves the destruction of Shacklewell Park.'

'Shacklewell Park? I don't think I'm familiar with...'

'You just spent the last hour discussing it... but really and truly you don't need to be familiar with the park to do this service for me. This next thing, you should definitely do,' I hold up the pen drive. I see him take his focus off me and train his eyes on the pen drive. Instinctively he reaches for it and reads the solicitors' embossed name on it. 'You should make a copy.'

From the breast pocket of his suit he produces a mini tablet, into which he plugs R. M. Laylor Solicitors' pen drive.

'You're looking at the file of Buki Nneka. She gave those papers to the solicitors,' I tap on the pen drive, 'as part of legal proceedings. It's all about Domain Management who were invited but did not attend your last meeting. The solicitors

changed clients and sold the documents to somebody else.
Probably Grayson Fielding.'

'How much of this can be proved?' The Deputy Mayor
asks circumspectly.

'Some of it quite easily.' I look back across the London
skyline. 'A lot of it proves itself, but what doesn't, I will be
able to prove by the end of the day.'

I smile at the Deputy Mayor who has gone very pale.

'Don't worry, if I were going to blackmail you I would
use the fact you're in league with a not very nice corporate
developer to sell the few remaining open spaces of the poor
parts of London to make a lot of money. I might not even be
alive by the end of the day, but whether that is the case or not,
I can assure you that nothing will be the same for Grayson
Fielding and his associates, when the shit hits the fan.'

I put my collar back down and I make to go back inside
the office.

'Mr Deputy Mayor I was going to stop the work on this
Shacklewell Park myself. I was thinking of disabling the JCBs,
stealing the guard dogs and dynamiting the sites and keeping
at it until it all got too expensive to insure.'

The Deputy Mayor smiles, thinking I'm joking, then his
smile disappears as he isn't sure that is the case.

'But I shouldn't need to do anything like that now. Right?

'Anything else you want me to do?'

'Yes. There is an Audi with this year's plates on it parked
down the road. Can you make whatever calls you can to stop it
from getting towed away, please?'

'And if I don't play ball? I take it that you'll go to the
media, right?'

'No.' I answer truthfully, 'We'll still be friends.'

By now I have broken the cardinal rules of negotiating.

'And Kelja?'

'Who's Kelja? Not a chick I know.' I smile before I take two cards from a box on his desk. I pocket one and write on the back of the other, 'That's my number. I take care of things that people don't need to know about. You'll need somebody like me. If there's a fixer you already use – I'm better.'

You don't wanna be missing – you might get found by somebody kissing!

Leaving City Hall I dial the number Roxanne had called again, but there's no reply. Back outside I begin to laugh. And why not? The police are looking for me, Cromber's gangsters will be looking for me soon and all I've really been able to do with my day is save a park when I wasn't trying to and taken the card of a politician who may only reluctantly take my calls.

Klu bowls alongside me, inspecting me curiously.

'You seen this bruv?' Klu says handing me a copy of the Evening Standard.

This is the reason I don't laugh much. I stop breathing and I take a look at the headline of the newspaper Klu holds in front of me that reads: *'East London Preacher Murdered.'*

The picture underneath has a caption that reads: *'Shot dead outside a nightclub in Canning Town.'*

Cromber was dead.

The news of his death affects me more than I would have expected.

It's not that I care, or because I had been with him just a few hours ago or that it wasn't expected or even a real shame. Predictable gangsters like Cromber are good to have around because I can stay out of their way if I'm smart, and I am smart most of the time. Now, there will be a fight for his turf. Mossi has to be the favourite but there are others in the wings who

154

also want to upgrade their car to a chauffeur-driven Bentley. I will have to adjust to the new top man. But this isn't why it has an affect on me. It is because Cromber is the third man to have died today, just after seeing me.

Carefully but quickly, I find my phone from amongst the three on my person and find the last text message I received from Fanny:

'THAT'S FINE. ONE HOUR AT THE CUT.'

It's ten minutes short of an hour since he sent this. It might already be too late.

'They're going to kill my Turk! And make it look like I did it.'

You don't wanna be missing – you might get found by somebody pissing!

'What's happening, bruv?' asks Klu as he hands me the keys to his Ford Focus.

'Somebody's contacted Fanny pretending to be me. He's where we meet sometimes. They're going to kill him.'

'Who?' Klu asks.

I hand my phone to him, 'Keep dialling this number!' before I answer Klu's question.

'Whoever killed Cromber and Edmondson... they might drive a grey Hyundai.'

Klu asks, 'What do they wanna kill Fanny for? Business?' Klu says that last word with extra excitement as the driver of a diesel engine tanker embarrassed at being overtaken by an obscenely orange-coloured hatchback sounds a booming horn at me.

'It's not about him but me. They want me to go down.'

Klu's staccato speech is stop-start as he listens to the phone ring but he continues because he needs to understand, and quickly. And also we're driving at over fifty miles an hour in a built-up area, in the daytime. He glances behind us every now and then to make sure we're not being followed. The best habits die hard. Certainly harder than a few people today.

'You think it's this Shampoo Crew?' Klu asks.

I want to dismiss the whole notion of this Shampoo Crew but how can I when I'm having the kind of day I'm having. But in amidst the improbabilities and craziness I focus on one incontrovertible fact.

'Bruv!' I head into Hackney proper, whipping past a bus trying to turn left out of Old Street. 'Is there any chance there can be a crew working London let alone Hackney called The Shampoo Crew that you and me don't know about?'

Klu shakes his head.

'These guys are taking lives so I take the rap and end up in prison. How badly would a crew want me to go down? To do all this shit instead of coming at me with sawn-off shotguns. I haven't pissed anybody off that badly! I'd know if I had done.'

I illegally overtake another Ford Focus which is doing at least sixty. It's not fun and games with the speed cameras this time.

'This is crazy shit! Them two dead girls last night, Cromber, your Buka chick that's missing. You think they killed Roacher too?'

'A popo.' I shake my head and straighten the wheels. I look at Klu quickly. He in turn shakes his head at me. His latest attempt to call Fanny hasn't worked. He holds the handset out on it's speakerphone setting, and we both hear the ringing sound and the phone go through to a voicemail or some other sound that isn't Fanny's voice.

At the junction in front of Stoke Newington Train Station we accelerate past the traffic lights on the wrong side of the road, causing commotion and loud car-horn protests. Klu apologises with a two-fingered gesture.

The road up to Stamford Hill is the most traffic free I can ever remember seeing it so I drop to forty-five for the right turn at the lights. At the small roadway that will take me down to Springfield Park I'm blocked by a motorcade of five Volvos waiting patiently behind the give-way lines. I drive past them and onto the grass of Clapton Common. The road from the Common down the Springfield Road is downhill.

Some maps call it the River Leigh. Other maps refer to it as Hackney Cut. The second kind are the maps we use and where it is at its quietest is where Fanny and I meet when one of his businesses doesn't afford enough secrecy. Moving downhill, I pick up speed and Klu's car gets bumped around less. As we swing onto the pavement tarmac we hear what might be a gunshot. Fifty quick metres later we hear what are definitely two more gunshots in quick succession.

I brake hard and Klu and I are out of the car and moving towards where the gunfire has come from. There's no strategy, plan or contingency or gun. We move as quickly and quietly as we can.

'Mensah!'

We take cover behind a wall. We can't see or hear anything. Bending low but keeping my head up so I can see as much as possible, I creep towards where there's sometimes a barge moored to bollards along the pathway. Klu follows.

Abruptly come the sounds I was anticipating. Four shots ring out. There's a blur of black and grey as gunshots echo and Klu and I dive behind recycling bins and a stack of black rubbish sacks.

'Are you hit?' I ask Klu.

'Nah! But this is fucked up though!'

The men responsible for the gunshots call out to each other in what sounds like Russian but isn't.

'Mensah!' they laugh now. Just as I start to think maybe Mensah means something in their Slavic-sounding language, one of them speaks English, 'Mensah! You're not fast enough!'

Then they're running away, while I can do nothing because there might be a man covering us to make sure his friends get away safely. A big engine roars and four wheels mash against the underused tarmac and speed off with the five men I've counted on board. All that's left is the sound of my and Klu's breathing and gunshots coming from the departing men.

You don't wanna be missing – you might get found by somebody fishing!

We run to the side of the river bank where Fanny and I used to meet.

'Look!' Klu shouts, before he jumps into the water. I kneel at the bank and drag out the man from where Klu pushes him. It's messy extracting him from the water. Fanny spits out a lungful of dirty water. Breathing hard and fast in a way that makes me think he'll live if he gets to a hospital straightaway, Fanny is grateful he's not in the river any more but now focuses on the bullet hole in his shoulder.

'It's okay man, you'll be alright!' I tell Fanny. I take my tie off and fasten it around his shoulder to stop the bleeding.

Klu and I ease him to his feet. Fanny winces but gradually starts to breathe better. Klu runs ahead to get the car.

Instead of concentrating on putting one foot in front of the other Fanny struggles to talk. 'I get message! They talk like they're you! You...' Fanny still struggles to speak, 'In... in van... the... the... Albanians!'

I keep Fanny's spare arm around my neck as we walk to the

edge of the green.

Klu spins his fast-moving car in front of us, pulling up with a screech. He jumps out and helps me put the wounded man in the passenger seat.

With sirens bearing down on us I tell Klu, 'Drive him to Homerton Hospital, but don't hang around, remember we were never there.'

I go from thinking Klu won't make it back to the nearest traffic lights before the police cars respond to phone calls of gunfire in the locality and apprehend his brightly-coloured Ford, let alone succeed in getting a half-dead Turk away from the scene of a shooting to Homerton Hospital.

I zig-zag through the surrounding streets on foot leaving behind the sirens and lights of the police cars and don't stop until Stamford Hill.

I look at the dark grey sky.

They've done their best to kill my friend Fanny. Turkish gangsters are the most reasonable kind of gangster I've ever known but when they make a decision there is no more negotiation and no quarter is given. I'm glad that the Albanians will shortly be experiencing the Turkish backlash for what they've done. They don't know what they've let themselves in for. I will find out who the driver of the Korean car is and where the Albanians are. Then I will find out who sent them and when I do, I'll have Fanny's family as very angry and unforgiving allies. And that's why I'm glad.

That should have your pants full of shit!

I sit sideways on a number 149 bus going in the opposite direction I sped down ten minutes ago. I must be in shock because I haven't been on a bus for nearly ten years.

People trying to kill me I can handle. People trying to send me to prison always give me a headache.

My phone rings.

GRAYSON FIELDING CALLING...

I look at the phone ringing. It brings into focus my frustrations at all the mysteries involving Fielding and his wife and his shadowy business dealings which stretch as far as City Hall. What makes matters worse for me is there is nothing to indicate he's more than the average bad man.

I look at the phone until it stops ringing. And then it starts again and because looking at it won't stop it ringing I take the call.

Silence, then, 'Mr Mensah.'

'Mr Fielding.'

'Have you any news for me?'

'I will have later. Everything is falling into place.'

'Perfect! My house in The Bishop's Avenue this evening then, at nine.'

'Probably better first thing tomorrow morning.'

'Seven tomorrow morning, then.'

'Fine, I'll be there.'

I resist the temptation to suggest seven should be nine in case it gave Fielding the impression I cannot get out of bed in the morning.

Rockin' your boulevards looking hard with our bodyguards...

I get to the barber's in Well Street where I have arranged to link up with Klu. His news about Fanny didn't seem very hopeful and I assumed the worst.

By the door is an African man, nearly seven foot tall and weighing a ton, looking down at me. He steps aside and lets me push the door open enough to walk in without touching him. I pull my trousers up a little from just above my bending knees as I sit. Mindful of the unfamiliar doorman I keep my hands out in the open and on brown leather on either side of my seat.

I forget what the barbers was called before but now its called The Head Doctor.

This barber's is the most upmarket of the five on Well Street. Nothing downmarket is acceptable here. I plant myself in the seat diagonally opposite to the only man actually getting his hair cut in a barbershop with a dozen-strong population. His eyes almost catch mine through the reflection but I look away. I'm not ready yet. Between us is a central walkway that takes weed smokers out through the back door and away from the wide window spanning the shop front.

I don't know exactly what I expect here, and how to ask for it. Trying to relax I breathe out quietly and out of habit look around willing myself not to see anything to cause me concern which I don't have the energy for. There's the betting-shop fly, a teenager all dressed in G-Star Raw®, who's officially the cleaner and is trying not to look like he's only been in Europe for a matter of months, who uses this place as his official work address for immigration issues.

It's then I notice Togolese Mike. I scowl at him and he sneers back. So it's here that I've seen him before. It's a mark of discernment when a man gets his hair cut on a Thursday knowing his scalp will be better rested in time for his weekend activities.

The only other thing to look at apart from the barbers and the Arsenal posters is the Black woman at the other end of the futuristic-looking couch that I'm sitting on. She's the same shade of dark brown as the couch which contrasts with her eyes that are a sort of dark green. Her make-up is an unlikely combination of green lipstick and light purple eyelids. She strokes that part of the Conya Doss style afro around her ear.

Her name is Genevieve Diop and she belongs to the man getting his hair cut, Benjamin Armah. She looks at him now and they have a conversation with their eyes. What his eyes say makes her smile but the barber swivels Armah around to face an impassive mirror. Genevieve goes back to flipping through a magazine of Rap video girls. Her brow furrows deeply at the outlandish bums and breasts – some God-given, others courtesy of the surgeon or airbrushing.

Benjamin Armah was always going to be famous when four far-right thugs jumped him in N1. Men armed for war beaten by Armah who had no street pedigree.

Some said Armah killed ten in total including a hit squad sent after him to Ghana. Others said it was none because the people he was supposed to have killed had actually been killed by the ghosts of his ancestors he'd used juju to call. I think I'm ready to accept help from anywhere including somebody else's ancestors. Mine have not been of any help.

With the public killing of white men that didn't like Black men the consensus was Armah had achieved the holy grail of crime and gotten away with it. People had probably got the details wrong about what had really happened, but they couldn't really be sure and neither could Armah.

He looks at me again only briefly, and then we both look away listening to the football talk and music-channel noise coming from the wall-mounted widescreen TV and the barber's supporting cast of pundits and critics.

The barber swivels his chair round so Armah is facing his woman. Then he's facing me again and there's no more looking away. The barber is almost finished now.

'I remember you,' Armah says to me. 'You were three years

ahead of me at Downside Primary School. Then you were Monica's boyfriend right?'

'I had been one of them,' I say.

Now he says these things, I remember him too. He had a mum and a dad. He was always smiling then too. He has a face disposed to smiling, it had got Armah out of trouble others wouldn't have survived even if his smiling face had got him in trouble in the first place.

'I don't see you about any more,' I say to keep the conversation going.

'I used to be about but I live in Ghana now, mostly…'

'What's that like?'

'Why?' Armah looks at me through the mirror on the wall. 'You thinking about making the move?'

'Maybe,' I say.

Armah doesn't say anything else for the moment.

I've never had a job interview but I suppose this must be what it's like.

'It's slow, hard and hot. And, it's real. The lazy need not apply. Every day tough new meat to eat. If you can't swallow you'll choke,' he says.

'You get that here, too.'

'Yeah but, Ghana hasn't spent hundreds of years robbing anybody so you come there and it's like, "We don't owe you shit!" ' He puts the quote marks around it by an African lilt in his tone like Aunty Merley does.

He could provide a good escape route and I'm grateful to Monica for quietly pointing me in his direction.

Klu walks into the shop. He's changed, wearing a new set of clothes including one of my exclusive seal jackets. This means he's broken into my house or visited the shop Dedei manages. Either borrowed or stolen, I'm unlikely to see payment for it, and neither would I expect it. Family. Klu, Dedei and Aunty Merley are the most normal people I know. This doesn't say much for them but it doesn't have to. They don't care what people think about them. I'll miss them if I have to go. I have to say it. Everybody else I'll think of but I'll miss the Adjeis. And Monica.

Klu passes by me without making eye contact. He's learnt that from me. No need to let a room of people who are potentially about to kick my arse know I've got an ally. It doesn't really apply here where we both grew up. Possibly, the mountain at the door makes him think.

I try and imagine the big man posing for a passport picture if he has one. He has literally been draped in Ted Baker by somebody else – I would bet on Ms Genevieve Diop. He wears clothes only because he's been told he has to. Everybody is naked to him.

The barber has finished and sprays around the perimeter of the fresh cut. Armah's face is surrounded by a cloud of scented oil. When the mist clears the bib around Armah's shoulders has been removed.

He's wearing a purple polo shirt and where I expect to see an under-or-oversized Ralph Lauren horse-and-rider logo on his chest there is instead an embroidered insignia of an elephant with an antelope sitting on it. Leaning back Armah adjusts his trousers at his belt. He like me doesn't wear his trousers ridiculously low. He's wearing brilliant white flip-flop sandals that deflect all suspicion and draw interest. Armah leans forward and looks around as if watching out for the next customer to move towards his seat. He scans the hangers on. His eyes settle on Togolese Mike, they narrow in distrust and dislike. I like his instincts. They are not the instincts of a Black man wearing white sandals on a Thursday in Hackney.

'If you have a particular set of problems, they don't stop being problems just cos you go to Accra! The Ghanaian government plays the bitch to the British government… immigration, extradition… certification.'

'Real talk!' Klu chimes in, this being a subject close to his heart. 'It's not the same if a British citizen commits a crime there. They pick up the phone and say it's not right that a Brit should eat African porridge what with the mosquitoes and Osei Tutu and all that! But if a Ghanaian gets busted here…'

Armah nodding finishes off, 'They don't give a fuck if Chief Kwrakranya himself of Accra calls – a Challey will serve his time here then they deport him!'

Armah looks at me, 'Problems just come dressed cooler. Then there's this Facebook and Twitter thing! It's a global village we're in now, for better or worse bruv.' He's still the most relaxed Black man I've ever seen without the chemical assistance.

'I'm not on Facebook.'

'Really,' Armah says impressed more than surprised. 'That's good.'

Gone are the cautious glances of few minutes ago. Even the barber walking between us doesn't break the eye contact Armah and I have.

There'll be none of my usual offended refusal to reveal interest. I have been doing things my way and I am having a supremely fucked-up day so I need to do things differently. I need Armah to know I'm very keen on any help he can give me to make it out of today alive.

We both clamber out of our seats.

'So, what you're saying is there's no point then?' I ask.

'No no no… all I'm saying is you've got to want to be there. It's not like here, with infrastructure and proper lines of enquiry and grievance procedures when things get fucked up.'

'I don't use either.'

'That's even better. A stay there as a UK undesirable might work for you y'knaa!' Armah's volume decreases but his intent increases. 'Don't get me wrong, there's still moves to be moved. I can get you on our continent, and the Home Office and border agencies don't need to know what they don't need to know.'

Genevieve Diop is uncomfortable with the subject matter. Armah holds the door open for her and she leads the way out.

'Get me on this number.' Armah hands me his card looking round again most concerned with Togolese Mike, 'I'm leaving tonight.'

The woman clears her throat.

'We're leaving tonight.' Armah says quickly. 'Expedited exit. The only way to travel when you've got big trouble coming... y'get me.' If I didn't get him, he was talking to the wrong kind of person.

Armah admires his haircut in the reflection of the SUV the big man at the door has the keys to.

'Still the best place to get trimmed mehn! In Ghana they take too long and use actual alcohol. They've got all the Dapper Dan fancy gels and juices but they use the alcohol just to see your eyes water.'

'How d'you figure I've got big trouble coming?'

'You're in a barber's... not trimming but getting other people's hair on your one... two-thousand pound suit... it's got to be a special kind of trouble... Kuvodu!' Armah shouts the name of his bodyguard or an African word for let's go.

The seven footer gets behind the wheel of the SUV and I feel relief as he drives away.

Gold comes to Hackney.

Using a circuitous route I make my way to Amhurst Road and Narroway looking out for police officers or their cars. I'm thinking about taking a trip to the airport to see if Buki has left the country on either of her passports. After the day I've had the answer must be in front of me but I can't see it... Buki Nneka's tattoo, the solicitors, Cromber, the threat on the iPod, Edmondson's high talk, Fanny's shooting... even maybe that suitcase.

The people that are lying or dying or both, then Buki Nneka and her rich husband, it might all be connected or that maybe the only connection is it's happening on the same day. I'm fighting completely different wars instead of just one and the weapons are different too.

Four of the five Holly Street Towers and their ubiquitous graffiti have gone, the estates are no more, replaced with the Nightingale two bedroom-house haven, now for only the most respectable of socially-housed tenants.

I get to Narrow Way, the spot where Armah had faced off the BNF. I sit on the circular bench under the rotating ad hoardings, finally taking a rest on this day that wants to frustrate and then kill me. I need chaos to be able to think and I'm only left with two places for that old Hackney flavour. Here in Central and Ridley Road Market.

I see a man watching me. Then he isn't. Tired, I rub my face and think hard. If my subconscious knows what's happening it hasn't seen fit to tell the rest of me. All I do know is my head hurts and nothing that seems to be happening really is.

The man isn't just watching me but coming towards me. I mouth an oath and instinctively turn and look around for an escape route. Across the road is another man with the same

167

kind of crew cut brown hair. There is another in matching gangster chic. I take a step up only to see more guys in matching patterns approaching from the north. I stand still. If they're real pros only one of them would have a gun.

I know the McDonald's doesn't have a back door, so surrounded, I wait. The man I saw last is the first to speak when they arrive.

'Come with us!' he sounds like they all smell... foreign. Even more foreign than me.

I'm grabbed by the shoulders and arms and marched down to Amhurst Road.

The men... the Albanians... I only saw fleetingly earlier have got me. The sky has gone a full shade of black in mourning for me.

There's a blue royal mail sized van parked across the road. It's there we're headed. My throat catches and I realise I have barely resisted at all. Not even to be polite. I hang a trailing foot. My marcher to the left swears as he trips on it and loses his footing only slightly, but before he can look at me disappointed with my attitude, I put a knee in his face. The others recover from my token attack and appreciate it in the spirit I intended it – a little something for appearances' sake. Not wanting to alert any onlookers they do nothing in response. Our pace towards the van has picked up mostly because of the man to my left who knows his nose is bleeding even without checking.

Two of them run ahead to open the back of the van. I see the empty yawning chasm inside, it starts raining. I try to resist further but the men are expecting this. Even before I can put one or both feet against the rear bumper one of them punches me on the side of my head and while I try to see and hear past the ringing in my head I'm pushed in.

One of them puts duct tape over my mouth, then a sack over

my head that scratches my face and feels like it's made from old rope or something similar. I am impressed. Local criminals would just as likely put pepper in my eyes or use a pillow case.

I feel plastic cable ties being pulled tight around my wrists. Just when I had started thinking that this was just a slightly more than usual fucked-up day in east London it really does seem like I'm supposed to die after all.

My heart is my enemy, urging me to panic. I stay in the recovery position and push away the thoughts that try to make me shake all over or freeze… not because either will help. I have already seen their faces. In the movies this means they're definitely going to kill me. I don't know what it means in real life. I only know about east London and here the finest criminals like you to see their faces just to see how you react. To see the look on your face every time they pass you in the street or when they check in on you to see if you're stupid enough to report them to the police.

I've never been a hostage. This isn't a kidnapping, kidnapping is when there is a ransom. This is an abduction.

I'm grateful. I haven't been with these men long enough for Stockholm syndrome to start but I'd started to think this day was going to end with me in prison and this is better. I still don't know why they didn't do this before. Maybe they did have reasons for killing everybody they have done and I'm just the next man on the list. Maybe it's still about me and all of today will be blamed on me and I just won't be around to mention to anybody that I didn't do it. It won't be my problem any more.

The only way I might be able to live through this is if I let these men know I understand men like them. I've met lots of men like them and had friends like them. I'm the last man to take it personally. I was a man like them. In the midst of it all

I wonder if the grey Hyundai is still following me.

I've stopped worrying about suffocating and wondering if and when my eyes will get used to the darkness. I'm good at noticing details but how long I've been restrained in the back before the van pulls to a stop is one detail I miss. I only note that it's raining harder than it was at the beginning of the journey.

They shout at each other and whoever's waiting for me. They lead me away from the van. I struggle to keep up, expecting to walk into a wall at any time and hoping it will knock me out so I don't have to feel what comes after. We're inside a room and their tones become quiet and questioning. We just stand, all of us, not moving. Then there are footsteps but not from the men that brought me here. Someone new.

One of the men says something in Albanian. I still hope somehow that he's saying, 'This is Nathan Mensah,' in their language and not, 'Is this where we should kill him?' I am very scared and I don't want to die after all.

They take the sack off my head. I keep my head down and remain calm. They have to be impressed.

'Well hello! Mr Mensah.' An English man with a familiar-sounding London accent exclaims. 'I'm so glad you have accepted my invitation to call!'

I'm punched hard to drive home the warmth of his welcome. With my hands behind my back I manage to keep my balance before I'm punched again. I look up after what seems long enough. I try to keep disgust off my face. I am going to be killed by a man named Patrick Fitz.

Play or get played
I glance around now, still braced. I won't look away from another punch.

'Silence is golden. Duct tape is platinum.' Patrick Fitz pulls the tape off my mouth, adding to the excruciating pain I'm feeling. He looks like he is enjoying my suffering. There are three men in the room with me. The third man in the room I don't know and isn't taking part. He's much younger than us, younger than Klu even, wearing the Klu-type roadman clothes. Black jeans, dark grey hoody under a green bomber jacket.

The second man is Mossi. He hides his broken arm inside the nice big coat he was wearing the first time I saw him today but not the second.

Fitz sneers, assessing me like a silver briefcase full of money, 'I do believe you're even more the picture of sartorial and criminal elegance than you were this morning! I hope we didn't interrupt anything important?'

Both of my legs have been tied to the front chair legs and my hands to the metal bar at the back of the seat. 'That's quite alright,' I say not showing any more surprise at seeing Mossi here than I have done at being abducted then punched in the face by the owner of a small record label. 'I was on my way here anyway.'

'You thought I was one of those white men you can scare off just because you're a big Black man!'

Fitz underscores every word with a punch aimed at my face. Why was he so angry? I'm the one getting punched. Mossi is laughing which makes more sense. I let the pain be at one with the abnormal flow of my day.

'You've had quite a day,' Fitz says sniffing long and hard. He's on something, quality cocaine probably, and I'm at his mercy. 'Where are the papers?' he asks.

'What papers?'

'The papers you killed my brother for!'

'What?'

'The papers you killed my brother for!'

'You've made a mistake,' I say licking my lips and closing my eyes to help handle the pain. 'I haven't killed any brothers for papers today.'

Fitz looks at me long and hard again. The same way he had when I had mentioned Grayson Fielding. 'Where have you been today and what exactly did you do there?'

I don't think about the question, just about what will save me and what I can say to keep me alive long enough to get the chance to kill Fitz and Mossi. The pain I'm in now means I would enjoy killing them. I always enjoy killing professionals and those who hurt me first, or try to. No guilt attached because they've chosen to step into my world in a specially deserving kind of way.

'Your brother,' I say without particularly thinking about it. Finally one shoe drops, and it and the other shoe are all I can think about. 'Edmondson... Edmondson?' I look Patrick Fitz in the eye daring him to react like a man not in control of the situation. My question was shorthand for I know he means the papers they had sent Edmondson to look for that he hadn't found or failed to hold onto. Papers that R. M. Laylor had placed on a handy USB for me and the Deputy Mayor of London to use.

I look again at the red eyes and nose. It might be that Patrick Fitz doesn't have a cocaine habit but that he's been crying over his brother. When Edmondson had fallen in on the safe side of the balcony and said brother, Klu thought he was calling me his brother. But Edmondson was calling on his brother who had sent him to look for documentation he wouldn't understand the import of.

'And your father is Grayson Fielding?'

Fitz hits me and every blow he lands on my face fits a piece into the puzzle... who they all are, where Buki Nneka is, who they all are to Buki and what they want in my town.

Fitz, who acts likes he has lost interest in what I did with my day is definitely going to kill me because accurate or not he thinks that's what his father wants and maybe his brother dying also hurts even if it's only because he's lost the ultimate dogsbody.

'Hit me some more!' I ask my tongue hanging out of my mouth.

'Oh,' Fitz raises an eyebrow, 'you like it?'

'No. I hate it, it hurts a lot and it's helping me hate you more. See, you're gonna kill me, Klu or Klu's mum or my Turkish friends or any one of three dozen other people will kill you or you'll fuck up here and I'll live then I'll kill you! All this is going to make me feel much better about it all.'

I laugh at him. Even with my blood in my mouth I laugh at Patrick Fitz.

'You think this is a game?' Fitz asks me.

'No, this was a new suit!' I explain. 'And I'm thinking of what your father will say about this mess. A man like him with a son like you. You're already too much of a disappointment to him.'

Fitz's face shows no emotion. 'Oh yes, because you know him don't you?'

'Of course. Me and him are...' I go to fold my index and middle finger together and remember I can't. 'We're tight! I was up at his place today. He wanted me to help him get some animal heads for his office... maybe yours. He offered me a painting: *Gassed* by Sargeant somebody. I said no. What would it look like? A Black man with white soldiers on his wall!'

I look at Mossi. 'I think he tried to call you, but your line was busy.'

I look at the roadman on the door. He still makes a point of not looking over here. I hear Fitz saying, 'You're trying to say my father had you throw his own son out of a window?'

He has given me too much information. The driver of the Korean car doesn't work for him or he would know I went to see his father today. How much do I tell him and how do I make sure that what I tell him keeps me alive.

I had, it appears, been sent chasing around London on a national domestic, the husband Fielding had been replaced by the son Fitz.

Fitz had sent the Albanians to kill Fanny, and then they had brought me here. Had they or maybe Mossi and the doorman killed Fitz's little brother on somebody else's orders, Fielding's? I could tell Fitz but that's not my style. The room had been emptied for my stay except for a notice board with a magnet holding maps, correspondence, invoices and charts. Not unlike what I had seen on the e-dossier being hidden by R. M. Laylor Solicitors.

The boy at the door is playing with a mobile phone, still minding his own business.

'My father couldn't afford for people to know about me. His first wife would have been most displeased. I was the accidental outcome of one of his dalliances in the Army.'

'You're telling me this... all of today has been some old-fashioned bullshit playing itself out?' So I'm being chased around London just to save Fielding's blushes.

A fire alarm klaxon goes off in my jacket. Fitz and Mossi are surprised at the interruption. I too am surprised I haven't been searched. The phone doesn't ring for long, seemingly cut off.

ONE MISSED CALL... LAURISTON.

And a voice mail message alert follows soon after. 'Ah, a telepho-graphic missive!'

'What a prick!' I think out loud.

Mossi punches me in the face. My hurt face shows its disgust. Fitz digs into my pockets.

'Who is Lauriston?' Fitz asks as he looks at the name displayed on my phone.

I answer, 'A white man just like you calling to tell me the voice left on the iPod is of a white man just like you!'

Fitz says, 'Ohh! You found one of my friendly threats I left for Lavinia and... I forget what the other one was called.' Fitz looks at Mossi and they both laugh. 'I always sent them one of those when they were being stubborn and thinking about not giving me what I wanted... Which all reminds me... I must send my European friends to kill everybody you know, all five of them. And not even a real mother in the bunch. We're like twins you and me Mensah.' Fitz plays on his own phone and every button he presses projects a new image into my head of Lauriston, dead like Fanny probably. Frustrated and looking at the ceiling Fitz shakes his phone in that way that never helps when you can't get a signal.

'Well I'm going to leave you with our friend on the door here.'

On that, Fitz leaves and Mossi follows him out.

'Don't kill him, I'm going to...'

I can't hear the rest. Whether it's because I'm losing consciousness or he's leaving the room, I can't say. I'm dizzy, seeing everything as a dark blur as I try to look around the room. Everything here is music related. I'm definitely in the base-ment or attic of Fitz Beatz Studio. Probably the basement since the signal is that bad.

Their boy at the door has stopped playing with his phone

and looks at me. This was the part where I appeal to the one who's heart isn't really into my ordeal to try and beg for my life. The joke is on me because they've obviously chosen him for a reason.

He hasn't joined in the beating but he probably has cause to hate me too, in his own way. I think back to my conversation with Mossi this afternoon and it occurs to me that he might be Tony's brother or another relation, like I was to Dedei or Klu.

I have to say something, but not before I blink back the pain so I don't sound like I'm begging, however he says something first.

'Do you know me?'

I think of the Acura, the Maserati and the Bentley outside Cromber's club and ask, 'Depends. What car do you drive?'

'You don't know who I am, innit?' The boy asks pulling a knife out of his sock.

'Here we go again.' I close my eyes, braced.

Lead from the back.

Mossi, with his arm in a sling, bowls back into the room and he doesn't look surprised to see me as he left me hands held behind me and legs strapped to each of the front chair legs. Mossi does look surprised that the boy at the door isn't there any more but before it can properly register, I ask, 'Is she dead?'

'Is who dead?'

'Is Buki Nneka dead?'

All the people I know that have died and will die after me, and I am still concerned about a woman I have never met.

'You know who this Buki Nneka was? You wanna know?' Mossi asks grinning. 'D'you know she was in the house? Millions of people know who this chick is… or thousands.

176

Most chicks like her? They turn up in Dubai as some Sheik's ho. Not even the bottom ho! Just any ho! And this chick gets a big-shot husband… gets this old dude to marry her, no pre-nup or anything! A millionaire, billionaire probably. Fuckin' Buki Nneka! I ain't just swearin' you knaa! I mean she was fuckin' Buki Nneka! She fucked me, she fucked Cromber, I think Tony fucked her, she fucked this Fitz cracker here more times, then she said no to fuckin' for money and business!? She could have just been a recruiter too y'knaa. Can you imagine! She was supposed to help those Polish girls get girls, move them into that Chelsea house for a time until we get the Polish boys to take them… but her conscience stopped her.'

Mossi shook his head, 'I thought she was a real hustla! Fuckin' Cromber gets the love thing for this chick, trying to protect her and shit! Fucking it all up! This new business is beautiful. When girls are the cargo… and it shits on the drug business money. Even better when they don't even know it. Whoever said slow dough is better than no dough is a muthafuckin' liar!'

I nod, glad that the story of my day is slowly coming together. 'Now you're with James Bond over there!'

'Nawh, I'm more like James Bond than that oyinbo joker!' Mossi takes a gun from his waistline. 'You know what this is?'

'It's a gun.'

'I killed those two women with this last night. Me, and not them Polski guys!' He breathes in deeply before announcing what seems like it might be his favourite part. 'This is the gun that I killed the bitch Buki with. I killed her first. The two oyinbo bitches saw me do it so they had to go too. No witnesses! I didn't like them anyway. They enjoyed catching and sending people over too much!'

Mossi shakes his head at the memory.

'Cromber had to go to make room for the new kingpin!' Mossi preens and then shrugs at the weapon, 'Maybe it was the same gun that killed your Turk's faggot son. Fanny was supposed to tear up Hackney looking for his son. You know, turn the clock back to the good old days when you and me were doing the runnings. With all the east at war we were going to buy up property for cheap all over, but it never happened. Fanny had gone soft.'

By we he means Fielding or Fielding and Fitz. Mossi wouldn't have the vision or money to speculate in real estate. Even real estate cheapened by a war that involved all the drugs trade and everybody it affected.

'Them boys don't even know I killed their two women.'

And Mossi doesn't know that Fanny maybe survived the shooting.

'They are still pissed off about that but not as pissed off as you would be if you weren't going to die today! You know what I'm going to do, Nate? Because of what you did to Tony and for walking around this manor like you're gangster number one... I'm going to rape that Dedei girl. They make a big fuss about rape in this country don't they?'

Mossi looks like inspiration hits him, 'I'm going to make Klu watch, then kill him too. I'll leave the girl alive though. You and Klu will be gone so what can she do about it? She'd have to find another gangster who would want her pussy then we'd kill him too...'

Mossi grins. 'Or she would get her best revenge by living well. But you know what I'm going to do first? First, I'm going to kill you... make it look like a suicide using the same gun and leave you in that Audi of yours, just like we did with the Roach pig!' Mossi continues quietly though, 'All that's about to happen! Unless you tell me where the guns are.'

'Eh?'

'The guns you took from Tony,' Mossi says, 'I know you haven't sold them. You're keeping them for yourself right? But when's a small-timer like you going to have a chance to use them? Give them to me and I'll think about...'

'You are such a bitch.'

'What did you say?'

'You're a bitch. I'm sorry but it has to be said! The worst thing is you're so much of a bitch you don't realise you're one. You need a crew of... foreigners. They're not Polish by the way but Albanians. It's probably a big difference to them. You should have learnt that before doing business with them and pissing them off every time you call them Polish. They're probably waiting for you to stop being useful as a tour operator around east London so that they can kill you too. Anyway, you needed Albanians to kill Cromber and you need them to bring me in and start rumours about The Shampoo Crew doing all your dirt.'

I pause briefly before changing tack. 'Your boy on the door there, he's not even around any more. You bored him. You've been saying you want me dead for such a long time and now you have your chance. You bored him and he left. He doesn't respect you! Nobody respects a bitch. And now you're rollin' with this guy and taking orders from him, just like you took orders from Cromber and just like you'll take orders from the Albanians when they're ready, if they keep you alive.'

Mossi's chest is heaving and the hand holding the gun flexes.

'And what's even worse still is that you want to make me a bitch too! Instead of giving me a cool last line like you thought up earlier you're doing this bitch thing of pretending that if I give you these guns you'll let me live when we both know I'm dead anyway… or is it that you're not allowed to kill me?'

'I'm a bitch?' Mossi breathes loudly. 'Me?'

'I'm alive ain't I?' I'm in an awkward position for nodding but I manage it anyhow.

Mossi walks toward me bringing the gun up. His anger is extreme like his surprise is when I kick the gun… but he doesn't drop it. He reacts quickly though and brings the gun hand back towards my face. Before he can cope with more surprise, I smash my forehead against his jaw and grab his gun hand with both hands.

I hear the big clasp of his watch click but his wrist and the grip of his gun don't give at all. Whether Mossi's muscle is steroids and narcotics enhanced or all gotten from honest gym toil, in either case he'll have a high tolerance for pain. I ignore Mossi's upper body and use my heel to hack at his legs until I hear something break. He howls loudly.

GBH with intent
Maximum Penalty: 5 years imprisonment and/or unlimited fine
Criminal Justice Act 2003, section 20

I exhale as the gun drops. He is still stronger than me but he's suffering. Grimacing, he dashes for the gun but he is never going to be fast enough to beat me. By the time he gets to his knees I've got the gun and swerve out of the way of a shoulder charge.

With the gun trained on him, Mossi stops moving and concentrates on cradling his arm. I hold my finger to his lips while I whisper an explanation I feel he deserves. I back my way to the entrance to await Fitz.

'I got your man on the door out of trouble. He called me about running a police stop and stuff he shouldn't have in his car. You know the type! One phone call and he owes me his liberty. He told me that's why he purposely asked to come in on this, so he can help me out if he gets the chance, or make sure I get a decent burial. And I think he probably wants your spot.'

Fitz runs in shouting, 'What's going on? Are you alright?'

'Not really. Someone keeps breaking things on him,' I say as I grab hold of Fitz, slamming his head repeatedly against the door he's just come in through before letting go of him. He falls to the floor.

'Fitz, get up,' I yell at him.

He stands and before his heels are fully settled under him I shoot him in the left side of his chest. He drops on to his left knee then right knee. He makes an ugly sound as his lungs cave in and he quickly stops breathing.

Mossi's eyes are closed.

'Get out,' I tell him. 'Go on get out,' I repeat, 'and take the white man with you.'

Mossi stops and looks back at me, wanting to know what I am doing and trying not to look grateful.

'The CCTV will show me carrying him.'

'All Africans look the same to the police. They'll probably think it's me with him.'

Mossi is the ideal player to leave out there. I know what he'll do next. He'll come after me and this knowledge will help me send other players after him as he does. Because I know where I will be.

I think things through while tenderly examining my injuries. I've got calls to make then to wipe both phone memories.

But first a message to Lauriston:
'WHEREVER YOU ARE – LEAVE!'
Then a phone call to Klu.

'Tool up. Red alert!'

'Yes,' Klu rarely says yes instead of yeah but he does now, and, 'where are you going to be?'

'The usual place unless you hear different.'

There's nothing left to say. I hang up.

My next call is to Monica.

Whose car we taking?

I meet up with Klu in Clapton Square Park. 'We have business in north-west Hackney,' I say instead of hello.

'If that business is catching up with your Albanians, I bet Fanny's boys already took care of them.'

'What?'

'They've carpeted all east London with questions. Every dodgy eastern European has had an Turkish gun in his face. They want who shot Fanny real bad!'

'Let's see what's left at north-west Hackney,' I say driving Klu's car again.

From under the passenger seat Klu gives me a new set of clothes including another seal jacket. 'The guns are in the back.'

'We still looking for Bugsy Neggar?' Klu is not calm and doesn't know this is all part of the search now.

'Mossi told me he killed her... and those two women from last night.'

'She's been dead all along eh?' Klu muses.

'No.'

'What?' Klu asks as if by rote.

'Buki Nneka is not dead,' I kind of repeat.

'How do you know?' Klu asks.

'I just know.'

'North-west Hackney it is then.'

From Accra with love…

To be one of two Black men wearing camouflaged urban-warfare jackets is not a good time to get caught carrying a small arsenal and wearing bulletproof vests especially with five dead bodies lying around. 'It wasn't us, honest,' wouldn't carry much weight with the police even though it was the truth.

Klu and I make our way through the small derelict estate soon to be bulldozed into extinction. We find the flat we are looking for. The door is left open with its locks smashed to smithereens. There is blood everywhere. I can't tell if Klu is relieved or disappointed that the work has already been done. Klu would have made my work his work too. I would not have felt happy about using Aunty Merley's son like that. Having Klu here would have made me quicker on the trigger because I'd have wanted all tonight's blood on my hands. Instead, it's at our feet red, sticky and dirty.

Three shot and one stabbed. The first one, I'd seen at Mare Street. The second one too. And the third and fourth, they were the men in the van. Before that, one of them had said, 'Mensah! You're not fast enough!' after shooting Fanny. He had been right, and he still is. None of us are.

These men need to be dead for what they've done today and what they've tried to do to me.

'So explain this baby naming thing to me again,' I whisper as we go in search of the missing fifth man.

'My first son is always going to be named Nii Addy!'

'By every woman?'

'Yeah.'

'So if you have a third boy by a third woman, he's going to be Nii Addy too? How would you tell them apart?'

'Nicknames! Like they add a papa or fio or use their Sabla,

their spiritual name, or an English name if you've got one of those. Or you can use the mother's name like Nii-Addy Letitia bi, Letitia's son.'

'Shh!' I hold a finger to my lips.

Klu falls silent.

We both hear breathing from behind a corner we round cautiously. A fifth man who had been shot in the back lies face down half obscuring a hatch cover. I don't recognise him. He must have been the driver of the blue van. He's been trying to hold in the blood that's pumping out of his body with one hand, while attempting to open the hatch cover with the other. Klu and I crouch by him, I am somehow grateful that he's still alive although my police interview alibi might not cover me for this one's approaching exit.

'The girl! Buki Nneka!' I ask, 'Where is she?'

'We kill no women. Only men!'

I've spent a lot of time talking today. That's a problem with being an independent. I'm always outnumbered, always outgunned.

The five Albanians are now all accounted for. There's not going to be any more talking. The Turks used guns with silencers or the police would have got around to caring about all the bullets fired in this area.

It suddenly occurs to me that we're not finished here yet. The fresh corpse at our feet is lying awkwardly. Now he's dead it's evident it's not because of extreme pain he was in but because of a chain he was lying on. It's a part of a big metal link from just under his torso. We see more of it and the rest of the chain when we drag the latest victim clear of the opening which the Turks hadn't seen or didn't care about. They had come here looking for five men and revenge, and with five men dead their interest ended where mine begins.

Klu and I look at the lock.

'You gonna use that weak lock breaker thingy you got?' Klu whispers.

'That'd take all day on this! And we don't need stealth.' I take a step back. And ready my gun. Klu does the same.

We fire into the cover around the lock until at least one of our guns goes click. After that, kicking in the wood around the intact metal is easy. Then I insert another magazine of bullets into the base of the gun and check the emptied magazine has been wiped free of all prints. I exhale again while Klu kicks at the hole we've created at our feet.

Using the most artful of burglar gymnastics Klu is first down. 'Shit!' He says while hanging off the edge, but his utterance at what he sees doesn't prevent him from voluntarily dropping inside the room below.

I follow. Inside is a big space with its walls hewn out of the building's foundations. There's a row of eight adult-type cots and bunks. Six of them have women aged between eighteen and their mid-thirties tied to the frames with plastic cable ties, dazed and unconscious. Two cots have young men in their late teens. Neither of the men are Fanny's son. He's gone, if he was ever here.

The room's only other contents are stale recycled bottles of water and white chamber pots with broken blue colouring around the rims. No chains. Just cable ties like I had been tied up with. I hadn't thought I would find where the people-traffickers kept their victims. Not like this. If Fanny's men had taken more time they would have found this place and maybe started to work out what had happened to Fanny's son.

There's something so half-arsed about the whole thing. Just human beings stinking of sweat and fear. They wake up one by one looking at the two masked men holding guns standing in front of them. None of them react more than to flinch away from the cold Klu and I let in.

I drop my gun and start cutting the plastic ties. The last woman who I free squeezes my gloves for a second. Blinking hard, she's more alert than the others. If somebody is taking bets I would place money on her being the first to get up and remove any money she can from the dead men in the other rooms.

Klu and I look at each other.

'Klu, the men upstairs. Take all their phones and any paperwork you can find. Then, we're done here.'

Sounding uncertain and looking as young as when I first met him Klu asks, 'Should we call someone?'

'We should.'

I know what he's thinking but I don't do the hero.

Soon we are back in the gritty compound entrance. And there's that blue van again. I prepare to set fire to it. It will make me feel good and blue vans never set fire to themselves and the noise it will make exploding is the best way to call the emergency services to this site.

Klu hangs around looking more mournful. 'You still think Bucky Nixer is alive? Or still in the country?'

'She is,' I don't look up from erasing the vehicle's identifying marks, 'and I know where she is. It's one of two places. I'll go to one. You go to the other.'

Klu asks, 'Should we leave the guns?'

'Why?' I reply simply, 'We didn't shoot anybody, and maybe one day we'll be caught with guns matching the ballistics of the bullets fired to free eight enslaved white men and women.'

I change the subject and hurry my friend.

'Klu, by the time, those people sort themselves out and

realise that they're free to leave, I want this van to be FUBAR.'

Klu's eyes get as wide as his goggles looking at the grenades I hold up.

'Where did you get those?'

'Tony gave them to me.'

'Did you kill him before he did?' Klu asks.

'No, and I didn't kill him after.'

'Where is he then?'

'I sent him to Malawi in the container the guns arrived in.'

Klu pauses as if trying to figure out whether he approves or not. He heads off to the front of the vehicle to scrape the vehicle numbers off the windows and engine and take off the front number plate. What he doesn't do, I will.

'What next?' Klu asks.

'What time is it?'

'11.30 pm or 11.45 pm or 12.00 pm.' Klu replies.

'Then let's go clubbing!'

Your favourite criminal's favourite criminal.

As I wait for Buki Nneka in the club I think about things… I think a lot anyway but now I try to think about me which I don't do so much of. As usual the noise is good for my thought processes. Cromber is dead. The Albanians killed him to please Mossi with the coincidental result that it limited Buki's ways out. Buki probably didn't know Edmondson existed, let alone that this dead junky had anything to with her husband. Where hadn't I gone that was important?

So I stand like a displaced lighthouse in another black suit in the second of Cromber's clubs. His club in Canning Town will be closed tonight as that is where he was killed and will remain so for at least a few days. Klu is at the third club in Marble Arch.

The place is full of twenty-and-thirty-something Black people who hadn't decided what they are yet. Children of African immigrants or Black British.

I know she's not already on the premises. But she will come.

'We kill no women,' the last Albanian had said. And I believe him.

'Buki Nneka is alive,' I had said and I believe it. She has to be. If she isn't, letting Mossi live might have been unnecessary. Not the worst mistake I've ever made, but a mistake all the same. But the CCTV of him with Fitz Beatz's dead body should put him on the police radar.

I can see my reflection in the highly polished mirrors Cromber used to make the club look double its size and filled with twice the amount of beautiful glamorous people. And here they are.

It is something Mossi said and also something Mossi hadn't said. Cromber warned me away from Buki. And Cromber is dead. Of all the reasons Mossi gave for wanting me dead talking about Buki was the strangest. I am surrounded by people that look like me, but I have a different purpose. I can't relax. I could try to pretend to be really like them all as I do most days, but I take comfort in the fact that they could try to do what I do but they would do it badly.

Then I see her. Buki Nneka. She's on the ground floor and I'm on the first. It's her in an Afro-Saxon-type hood cloak. The getup should have been obvious but with the waist-length weave, and glow in the dark make-up she actually blends in.

The protesting sounds people make as I barge past them are what they'll be making all night. As I go I remove the luminous armband with spurious bouncer ID and white wire earpiece. As long as I'm just another brother I'm free to harass a sister as much as I want.

At the top of the narrow winding steps that will take me to Buki I see another girl. I recognise her and she recognises me. That insolent mouth and outrageously big backside. She was with Mossi earlier today. So Mossi is either here now or he soon will be. I could approach her but that would bring with it a whole new host of incalculable variables. It can't be helped. I can't lose sight of the woman I am here for.

I hear people within my earshot recognise her too.

'That's The Key!'

'She's The Key!'

'Buki Nneka!' I call.

Buki looks at me as if I've just called her Irene Adler. Maybe she's used to being called The Key or you're that girl aren't you, by those who know her from Facebook like I know her from Grayson Fielding's file. She'll always be Buki Nneka to me. I take hold of her arm and she looks at me. I'm almost surprised she feels real. She's also really angry.'

'I want to see Cromber. I'm going to tell Cromber!

She makes to shake my hand off.

I tell her, 'Cromber's dead.'

I tighten my grip and her eyes widen.

'You have to come with me.'

'He's dead?' She asks, 'Cromber's dead?'

'Cromber's dead,' I verify for her. 'Mossi is in charge now.'

Buki looks shaken by the news. Then she tries to run.

'It's okay.' I hold onto her waist and pull her back. 'You'll be okay. You have to come with me!'

In reply her nails ratchet across my face. I tuck my neck in and her second pass misses me. I can't let her go. I think about letting her run then merely following her out. But she'll run into the big arms of a never-go-down bouncer until the police arrive as they will tonight.

I cover her mouth and carry her the five metres to the ladies toilet. I wince as she kicks at my shins and elbows my ribs. It's a predictable indictment on modern urban society that no one tries to save her. All day I've searched through her life and I haven't stumbled on anyone who might be thought of as a friend of Buki's. There was Cromber but he's gone now.

One of the people on her Facebook page pictured with her might perhaps be a friend but with the enquiries I've been making about Buki, a friend would have got in touch at least to tell me to fuck off. But here she is, alone, being dragged to the club's toilets with nobody to help her.

We get to the toilet and the doorway is too smooth and modern for Buki to get a hold of anything which will prevent me from pulling her in. An attendant sits there, looking at us. Buki's defences have lost their initial ferocity but we still look a strange pair. I grip Buki close and she buries her face in my chest biting me. Gritting my own teeth I take out my money clip and peel off a fifty pound note.

'Give us five minutes!' I say to the attendant, 'Don't let anybody in.'

The woman takes the money, looks at it then at the clipped wad and at Buki. Buki has lost one of her shoes in our journey so she stands lopsided and angry. The toilet attendant looks back at my wad.

I remove another fifty from it and hand it to her. 'But if anybody comes in here I'll kill you!' I return the clip to my pocket. It says a lot about the calibre of the sort of people I've been dealing with today that this is only my second bribe of the day.

'Sorry! Out of order!' the old woman tells the young women wanting to follow us in.

I notice Buki isn't lopsided any more but I haven't asked why. Then she attacks me with the point of the heel of her remaining shoe.

'No there's no time!' I take the shoe from her and cuff both her wrists with my right hand. It's not enough to stop Buki hitting me but I can hold her close enough that she can't hit me anywhere where it will hurt. I let her go and she stops, still stunned. I size up the window as I throw her last shoe out of it. The window is too small so that nobody can get into the club for free, and also won't let anybody out either.

'I won't do it,' Buki says, making an assumption about me like I've been making about her. But that's not necessary now. I'm right here to tell her who I am and explain what I've been doing.

However, she repeats, 'I won't do it.'

'We have to leave before Mossi gets here,' I say, thinking about how we could get out of the building, because things are going to get seriously dangerous and unpredictable when Mossi gets here.

'You... don't work for Mossi?' Buki asks.

'No. I drive an Audi.'

'So, what do you want?' Buki breathes easier.

Buki's eyes are wide, even as they blink, 'But you don't work for Mossi... Are you some sort of fan?'

'Well, sort of...'

'Just a crazy fan...' Buki wants me to be the kind of menace she knows and understands, but I'm not.

'Mossi's people. They are looking for you. He's going to be coming here. I want to keep you safe!'

Buki is not convinced. How can she be? She's lied and been lied to so much. She has nothing else though, including fight. We leave the toilet less than the five minutes agreed, but I don't request anything back from the £100 I gave the attendant as we pass her. I pull Buki by the hand and she and I wend our way past the dancers in full flow.

'She's The Key!'

'The Key!'

'That's The Key!'

The time for posing is over and even people waiting at the bar are adding to the ripple of bodies innocently getting in my way. I lead her quickly to the front doors expecting no trouble until I get there. The important thing with clubs with metal detectors out front is that I know the men in the club don't have any guns, and the men waiting outside for me know I won't have mine.

I don't know if the club we leave behind was especially warm or if it's fear that makes me shiver slightly as the fresh night air assaults my senses. But it's cold out here.

'That's Mensah!' someone calls out.

'Mossi!' Buki shrieks.

Mossi's voice comes from a car in front of the bouncers and smokers who are ignoring Buki and me.

The gunfire starts before the sound of braking, and continues as Buki stops trying to pull away from me and we duck down. A second driver and a second gun enter the fray, moving in the opposite direction to the cars moving towards us.

The Bentley, Acura and Maserati that I remember from earlier, cut each other off and block their way out and the path towards me.

Speculative gunshots ring above and behind us as Buki follows my lead and shelters behind a white van that I'm equally glad and disappointed isn't a police vehicle. The shooters can't get us in their line of fire from where they're positioned.

DIALLING... KLU

'Klu, bring guns!' I shout a word that's a big no-no into the phone. I don't care that I'm breaking my own rules. I'm very angry that the Black gym monkeys want to undo all the work I've done and I don't care who knows it.

Today, I've seen a lot, heard a lot and done a lot so I must have been moving fast but not as fast as I do now.

I took the precaution of placing puncture kits in front of the tyres of all the flash looking cars but I haven't been able to cater for the roving mercenaries the girl with the lips called in. However secluded the parking spot there is no such thing as a place to park which is not known by all and sundry in this part of London. What would have been an L-shaped run to my car has now become an S-shaped one if not a figure of eight.

We get to my car. Buki doesn't know it's my car until I point at it.

'Sorry,' I shout. 'Quickly!'

With a heavy flick of the wrist, my hand holding her hand, I swing Buki to the passenger side door. She gets in, accompanied by digital beeps as she tries to dial the police. I don't have the number for the phone she's using.

'Here,' I take it from her, 'use this one!'

And she does, 'Hello! Police! Someone's trying to kill me... kill us! I think his name's Mossi,' Buki blinks, 'Please help!' She thinks she's calling the police but she's only making a recording I'm going to need later.

'Who are you?' Buki asks slowly as my car starts to move fast.

Like me, she has seen Mossi behind the wheel of one of the cars. She might recognise or know the names of the other two, and she also knows I don't work with them, not right now at least.

I look around not believing there are men in fast cars seconds away around the corner while I'm here answering her slowly-asked questions.

'I work for Grayson Fielding.' I talk fast but formally as if Buki might not recognise the name of her husband. I am working for Grayson Fielding, or am I?

Buki Nneka looks more confused at this than at anything else that has happened within the last five minutes. As soon as my car engine starts up, the sound of angry cars appear as if by magic.

I throw the car into gear but even as my car obliges taking me to fourth gear and fifty mph an Acura pulls alongside with little effort. A driver I don't recognise is able to pull a gun out and train it on me as we move. Open-mouthed and frozen I press down hard on the brake pedal. Buki's forehead hits my dashboard. The car with the gunman at the wheel disappears ahead, then a second car overtakes me with wheel-shrieking reluctance.

A car brakes hard behind us but still hits us as it slows down.

The two cars in front are quickly repositioning themselves but I steer past them. Maybe she knows whether he was driving the second or third car. A Bentley and a Maserati. It's all a blur to me.

She looks at me when I take away the phone I've given her.

'Will the police come?'

'Probably.' I take one look at the still distant following cars and prepare to slow down, 'But not now.'

The driver of the car furthest ahead has cottoned on to what has happened as I pass him and he's able to accelerate in the right direction, but not fast enough.

My car slides past at speeds that don't seem plausible in the short distance involved, and I'm gone, leaving them far behind and getting further away.

'That's why the Audi, bluhd!' I shout triumphant and more relieved than I realised.

Careless driving
Maximum penalty: fine and penalty points and/or disqualification
Road Traffic Act 1988, section 3

Hit and Run/Fail to stop/report motor accident
Maximum Penalty: Fine, 10 penalty points and/or 6 months imprisonment.
(Road Traffic Act 1988, s.170(4) 127)

A figure on a red motorbike speeds toward us. I recognise the motorbike and even without seeing under the black helmet I know its Klu. I know its Klu because between the time I called him and now is about how long it would take him to get here on a nippy motorbike like the one he's on from Cromber's other club doing a cool eighty mph. His journey through built-up areas doing more than twice the speed limit means the police are definitely on their way now, if they weren't already.

He doesn't look towards us but it's as if Klu knows that Buki Nneka is here with me, and he's showing off for her dark brown eyes. After he has zipped past he stops the motorbike across the width of the road so that he can balance and fire the two guns he pulls out simultaneously. Klu doesn't throw me a gun like he's supposed to but instead shoots behind me at whatever car is unlucky enough to be in the lead.

I pull up my handbrake and spin the wheel. Throughout our semi-orbit Buki never takes her eyes off Klu as she tries to figure out whose side he is on. I smell Buki's perfume.

If this was the movies every shot would count. The first

would shatter the Maserati's windscreen blinding the driver, the second shot breaking the windscreen killing the driver. Shots from his second gun would make the two wheels on either side of the car explode and send the car into a wild flip over Klu and crashing beyond my car. The Acura behind would brake hard and Klu would make it explode too. The Bentley in third place would brake and steer hard to the left to avoid the fireball the car in front has become and would crash through the embankment boundary into oblivion in the Thames.

But none of those things happen. The Maserati's driver brakes aiming his car at Klu, the wheels lock on the cars following us and they're going too fast to stop straightaway.

Instead of jumping off the bike and running, Klu treads concrete on both sides of the motorbike as the Maserati clips his back wheel. The impact with the motorbike is enough to slow the big car further. It gives Klu a point blank view on the driver but he's more concerned that his left leg isn't crushed.

There's no romance because this isn't a movie. These are east London criminals plying their trade in the West End. His two wheels clear Klu peppers all the cars. Then I don't hear a click or hear Klu swear as he runs out of bullets but I do hear sirens as we run out of time.

I realise I've been sitting inactive while Klu has been buying me thirty bullets' worth of time. I regain my wits and I press down hard on the car horn as I move off again. I hope Klu won't get himself arrested checking that the three unwise monkeys are dead.

I first go left and next move right zigzagging in and out of the streets of central London without getting any police attention. Euston Station behind us, I see the front of the Bentley in the distance. Better them than the police. I'm sure I won't get shot at again tonight.

Minutes later with Klu a couple of car lengths behind I pull into a building site of half-built apartment blocks. Klu gets off his motorbike, letting it fall on its side. He takes off his helmet and throws it down. Klu ejects both guns' empty magazines and takes fresh ones from his pockets. He gives me a gun after reloading it, then does the same for the second. Klu chooses the most dangerous times to be well-prepared.

Almost on cue to receive a shower of bullets the Bentley screeches around the corner. Klu and I take aim and fire. The car reverses, hard. I count at least ten bullets that hit home.

'Nigga!' Klu exclaims after another temporary triumph, we both turn to see Buki cautiously edging out of the passenger seat and looking at our guns. 'This chick has got you chased by three whip fleets now?'

I ask Buki, 'When was the last time you saw your husband?'

'Two hours ago.'

'Where were you at eleven this morning?' I ask.

'At our house. It's in The Bishop's Avenue.'

Fielding didn't bother to get the person I am supposed to be looking for out of his house before I came. He really didn't expect me to live any significant amount of time after I'd received that not insignificant amount of money from him.

'And Fielding was there too?' I asked her.

'Yes, probably, maybe,' Buki replied.

I've laughed already today, I can't remember when but I laugh again so that probably... maybe some good comes of today and not just my continued existence.

I look around and at the other end of the close I see an exit blocked with one of the barrier's emergency services are supposed to have keys for but never do.

'Here,' I take Klu's gun from him and hand Buki over to him. 'Take her somewhere safe.'

Klu thinks deeply on the matter then asks, 'Where?'

'Somewhere safe!' I begin to anticipate the return of Mossi's boys. 'Stay with her until I phone you.'

'You gonna be alright?'

'Course I will!' I point out that I'm holding a gun.

'B…' Klu protests.

'Go! Go!'

Hoisting up her dress to get astride the bike Buki looks at me, wild-eyed, but obediently gets on the back of the bike. She holds onto the back of her seat but as Klu starts up the loud engine she quickly binds her arms around him. I always envied Klu his easy relationship with his mother but I don't remember being jealous until now.

Before I can say anything else to either of them, they've gone past the barrier.

Mossi will be here soon. Klu will establish what they call in sports TV commentary an unassailable lead.

I push my car door closed, pause and take a proper look around me for the first time. I'm in Camden. Specifically, I'm in a new housing development with only a couple of show apartments finished. None of the fifty expensive apartments are lived in yet so the face-off can be here.

This is the kind of community that is very welcoming to the kind of resident who can and will call the police and be listened to. The police coming here on a what-the-hell-is-going-on call would make things here even more chaotic and chaos can be the best ally of the outnumbered. This is definitely as good a place as any. There's even plenty of scaffolding to use as weapons. I take one last look at my Audi, running a finger along the warm bonnet and leave it out in the open and go.

While I'm looking for a good position in a ground floor apartment I hear an engine. I run to where I can see an expensive motor roar up. Klu has evidently disabled the other two cars because all three men have got out of the one Bentley. My Audi's running lights shine on three men patrolling the area around it like a pack of animals. They've also left their lights on.

I left my car there as bait but I didn't expect what happens next. Setting fire to a man's car is as personal as it gets for a man who has no wife, girlfriend or children. I feel a pain in my chest. I've barely had the car for a week yet we've been through such a lot. Mossi with his hand in a sling is even carrying a petrol can of his own.

I fire a shot in the air and shout at them. I go through the whole spectrum of insults. As the situation dictates, they turn away from my car as I had expected and run toward me. I try to control my breathing as my heart pumps overtime.

At least one of them finds the apartment I'm in quicker than I expect but he moves slowly. He creeps in holding a gun and looks left, right and behind before each step. He's either more professional than he looks with the jewellery and all, or he's afraid of the dark. He should be.

He hears the racking sound of a police baton extending to its full length. He reacts, but not fast enough. He howls as I swing it into the back of his knee.

Assault occasioning actual bodily harm: 3 counts
Maximum Penalty: 5 years imprisonment and/or fine
Offences against the Person Act 1861, section 47

I don't wait to see if he's been knocked unconscious before I step over him and drive his head into the floorboards a dozen times, then I check that he's unconscious. He is, so I take his gun.

I hope Mossi isn't the next man through the door a full minute after his boy has been dealt with and he isn't. The second man is an able-bodied man who could make a pain of himself while I'm taking out an already handicapped Mossi. This way the man with two working arms takes a baton to the gut, loses his gun and is thrown against the wall and trips on a well-placed length of scaffolding. By the time Mossi can ready himself I have a gun trained on his face.

'You again! I thought we made a deal...'

'What deal?' Man two and Mossi bawl in unison.

I look at Mossi with an exaggerated look of confusion. Man two gives himself a DIY massage. We both look at Mossi and I continue, 'After what you did, give me one good reason not to kill you. If it wasn't for the deal we made...'

Mossi has more than one thought and tries to speak them both before I interrupt with the gun I've taken from one of his boys.

'Let me tell you both a story... There was a mongoose getting chased by a lion. In the middle of the chase the mongoose hides under an elephant and just as he's passing under the big boy, splat! The elephant does a wicked shit and covers the mongoose head to toe with some foul smelling but fresh shit. But hold on here comes the lion. He doesn't make the connection. Why should he? Piles of elephant manure must be as common as dog shit in Hackney and it's never had his lunch under it before so he doesn't check. In fact he walks... or strides or ambles or whatever the fuck a lion does right past the stuck-in-shit mongoose. The lion looks for a while longer then moves on! The mongoose cannot believe his luck. He jumps out of the pile of shit, singing and dancing, and cleaning the shit off himself. He's stolen victory right from the mouth of defeat! But suddenly, the lion comes back, and eats him all up. You know what the morals of the story are? Morals, plural? I haven't taken up all your time with a story that only comes with one moral. This has three! Moral one, not everybody that shits on you is your enemy. Moral two, not everybody that gets you out of shit is your friend. Moral three, when you're up to your head in shit keep your mouth the fuck closed!'

I don't usually talk so much. But I'm angry right now. It must be the car.

I put the gun on safety and after a second thought take it off safety again. 'Help me make this executive decision, should I kill you boys here for wanting to kill me? Are you not my enemy?'

'Do what you feel man!' Mossi says.

Man two mimics Mossi's upturned jaw but without the pious veins in his temple. I talk to him now, 'Go. Take your boy in the kitchen. He's resting.'

Mossi tries to say something, cry or laugh but it comes out as a cough. I see nothing but fear in his eyes.

'Can I have your car for Dedei, to compensate her for the loss of earnings you have caused her?'

'The Bentley?'

'Of course the Bentley!'

'So, it's a robbery ting yeah? If I don't give it up you kill me?'

'No-no-no! Why does everybody think I'm a gangster? This is not a robbery! This would be an act of goodwill.'

'Where's Buki?' Mossi asks.

'Who?' I ask him back.

'Where is she?'

'You said you'd killed her, didn't you?'

Mossi looks away, 'Watch out. When she starts playing that innocent thing you're about to get shot.'

I think about how strangely impressed I was by what Mossi said about Cromber and his feelings for Buki. I respected Cromber a lot less but I liked him a lot more. All that talk and he had fallen for Buki Nneka just like a lot of African and non-African men. I think he would be happy too with the way this is panning out.

'Give me your jacket,' I say to Mossi admiring his jacket, 'That's a robbery.'

I try it on. I don't have the muscles Mossi had it tailored to show off so I know the jacket will be happy to be able to relax around me.

I play with a phone I've taken from one of the pockets in the jacket that was Mossi's. 'That girl of yours from outside Cromber's club today, the one with the Chinese eyes and ridiculous lips. What's her name? The one who called you when she saw me tonight, what's her name?'

'Rochelle.'

'Rochelle. Very nice! She looks like a Rochelle.' I pocket his phone, now mine. 'I'm going to call her.'

Mossi spits, 'You think I give a fuck about her? Nigga please!'

'Maybe not but you'll give a fuck when I work through all your women.'

'Rape them all bluhd!' Mossi scoffs.

'Not rape. I don't do rape. They'll come with me by choice. Because they want to and have forgotten you.'

I place my finger over the trigger of the gun pointing at Mossi, 'So how d'you want this? Do you want to get in my car the easy way or the difficult way?'

You're gonna need a bigger boot!

I'm making good time down Amhurst Park when Klu and his motorbike come alongside matching my speed. I pull over at Stamford Hill. Klu leans over the passenger side window.

'Where's Buki?'

'You know you get into trouble without me...' is how Klu starts his answer.

'Bruv, I've spent all day looking for her.'

'Don't worry.'

'Where is she?'

'Trust me!' Klu says. 'So where we going?' Klu again takes advantage of a time when I have to focus and can't argue.

'Hackney Wick. The Olympics site.'

'Lead the way!'

Our small motorcade speeds through Hackney's familiar streets. We drive down through N16 past E5 and toward E9. The only incident is a bus driver's annoyed horn as I overtake him on the right and Klu overtakes on the left. We aren't racing, but we aren't dancing either.

As we drive past the old mental hospital I see the grey Korean three-door following me as carefully as it can. I have no reason to assume that somewhere between the police and the gangsters I've done enough that I shouldn't be followed any more, but I do.

Drawing Klu's attention I make a closing and opening motion with my thumb and index finger. Pincer. Klu's helmet nods. He snaps his handlebars around and taking the pavement, he speeds back the way we've come. I take my foot off the accelerator but don't brake so it takes the Hyundai driver a second or two longer to realise I'm slowing down, not seeing any brake lights. By then Klu is behind him and I'm beside him with my gun out.

'Come out slowly!' I say to Togolese Mike.

'Don't get excited!' He says, panicking, 'I can explain! I told Roacher I wasn't a snitch!' he shrugged. 'Then he asked to see my passport so I had to tell him what I know. It's what I do. I get information, except about you two. You two saw straight through me, I saw that! I made up the thing about The Shampoo Crew.'

I don't look at Klu at this revelation about The Shampoo Crew.

Togolese Mike shrugged guiltily, 'I thought it was funny. On account of their shooting policy: Aim for the head and shoulders: Buss'N'Go! You know I'm trying to be a rapper too.'

He looks at us. We're disgusted that he should try to make a joke as much as we're disgusted with the man himself. I'm insulted that Fielding would put this pathetic little man in the same league as me.

'You're a snitch and not a good one,' I make a point of saying.

'You're right. I'm just full of bullshit. I'm not even from Togo man! I'm a loser! You saw that too huh? Fielding did. At first I didn't understand why he wanted to hire you! Because it was me that found Buki the first time in that house in Chelsea! It was me that spotted how girls seemed to disappear around them. That wasn't what I'd been sent for but I notice that kind of thing! Girls who are there then not... men too sometimes! I told Fielding all about it but he still gave you the third job he had.'

'What was the second job he gave you?'

'See, what happened was, after I found the Buki girl, I got talking to one of those Albanian girls.'

'The ones that were making men and women disappear?'

'Mostly women. Fielding paid me to take them to a club in Canning Town. That's when they met the man from the studio.' Togolese shook his head at a painful memory. 'These white people are crazy!'

'And your third job?' I ask without needing to ask.

'Following you,' Togolese puts simply. 'Telling him where you are and where you've been and where you're going.'

I point at my car. 'Open the boot and get in!'

Mike hesitates.

I say, 'Get in or I will kill you!'

Threats to kill
Maximum Penalty: 10 years imprisonment
Offences Against the Person Act 1861, section 16

'Where you taking him?' Klu asks curious. 'Why not do him here!'

'He's going in the boot!' I say, unsure if there's going to be enough space. Klu, Togolese Mike and I look at the man already tied up inside with cable ties and duct tape over his mouth.

'Who's that?' Klu asks.

'It's Mossi innit!'

Klu, against my better judgement, removes the tape across Mossi's mouth freeing Mossi to shout, 'I'm going to kill you! Then use juju – bring you back alive and send you to the north and Burkina Faso and I'll pay a poor village of Hausas to stone you to death!'

There's definitely space enough next to Mossi. I point the gun at Togolese Mike again and say, 'Get in!'

Where there's a 9 mil – there's a way!

'Okay,' I shout. 'Here's the situation. This is the gun that killed two women not that long ago.'

I drop it in and it makes a resounding sound on the metal floor of the shipping container. It doesn't echo all that much because the shipping container isn't empty because it has me in it and my Audi with two men stuck in the boot.

I drop the other guns I have accumulated today inside as well, making more noise but again with minimal echo.

'I'm gonna leave these here.'

I hold the phone that formerly belonged to Patrick Fitz, but which smells of Buki now and her fear. 'This is a phone that has a recording of Buki Nneka crying in fear of her life and what not. I'm going to call the police on this phone and leave it playing for them outside. This container you're in was booked by a non-existent company owned by another non-existent company but will have something to do with Patrick Fitz, some dead Albanians I don't know the names of and possibly Grayson Fielding.'

I walk towards the entrance and I raise my voice so the two men sharing space in the boot can hear and there's more echo this way. I shout, 'The police are coming!' I ready two devices that are also present, evidence of the commission of a kidnap of one Buki Nneka.

'Whichever of you gets caught in the vicinity is at worst, going to jail, then maybe deported afterwards, or at best, has loads of questions to answer before getting deported.'

Outside, I lock up, depositing the secure bolt in its place across the two doors. I press the remote and I don't hear the boot door swoosh open so much as I hear two men struggling in a hard fought fight against each other for air.

I make sure I can hear the police dispatcher trying to communicate with the recording Buki didn't know she was making tonight. I place the phone carefully on the ground outside the container and hope it won't get smashed by a careless policeman. Next to it I place Mossi's and Togolese Mike's phones, which hold plenty of information on calls to and from men who are now dead, or soon will be.

Fearing one of them would get out and start shooting through the wall of the container, I run the half kilometre to where Klu is hiding behind the large piles of bricks and tubes.

'Nicely done my nigga!' Klu says watching and admiring through binoculars I removed from my boot to make space for today's guests. 'Kinda cold though, putting Togolese Mike in as well, when Mossi's the killer.'

'Yeah,' I agree.

I knew it would end here when I saw the location and container numbers in the file we stole from Buki's solicitors, who had in turn become Grayson Fielding's solicitors.

'How did you know Buki Nneka would be in one of Cromber's clubs tonight?'

It's the first time he's pronounced her name right.

'Why? Are you disappointed she wasn't at the club you were at?'

'No.'

'I've been looking for her like she's missing.'

'Cos Fielding said she was!'

I nod, 'So I've been looking for her like she's on the run or she's been snatched. But what if she hasn't run away or been snatched? What then? She wasn't missing. Doesn't know she's supposed to be missing. What if she's just been living life?' I shake my head not so much at how crazy this all is but amongst all the lies I've been told and circles I've gone in because of them… my day hasn't been misspent at all.

'This whole day was about Fielding keeping me where he could see me until he told the Albanians it was my turn.'

Klu marvels, 'Mossi? I would never have thought it! Mossi exporting them new slaves from London and perpetrating proper homicides on the road… and killin' them two bitches…'

'He didn't kill them.'

'But you said…'

'I said that Mossi said he had killed them. Not that he actually did!' I take the night-vision set from Klu. 'He didn't,' I conclude simply.

'How do you know?' Klu asks. I can feel him looking at me as I look through the goggles.

Slowly I answer him, 'The same reason I knew Buki was still alive. Because whoever killed the other two would have killed her.'

'So if he said he did but didn't, who killed those girls then?'

'I did.'

Murder: 2 counts
Maximum Penalty: Mandatory life imprisonment
Section 269 of the Criminal Justice Act 2003

Klu nods. He doesn't ask why, not today. I tell him anyway.

'They wanted to take Dedei,' I state. 'Those Albanians were going to have her in a place like that run-down estate we went to. They said her price was already going up on some site on the dark web. They were trying to make Buki work with them taking a whole lot of girls like Dedei from our area. I went to the house that night, in Brownswood, I told them who I was, and what Dedei meant to me. The first girl I shot… she laughed. She wasn't scared, she had the other girl and whoever she thought could protect her from me.'

Klu meets this with silence and has nowhere to vent his anger. I don't know what it feels like to have a brother or sister but Klu and Dedei are the closest I'll ever have to those things. I know they and Aunty Merley are the only reasons I would knowingly risk my life or liberty.

We watch the shipping container stand stock-still stoutly refusing to give us the show I had predicted.

'But he had the gun? Mossi!' Klu wants to get as many of the details of the story as he can in his head before putting them in order of the most unbelievable.

'Yeah, I left it,' I shrug. 'Mossi happened on the scene after the fact. Picked up the gun. He was working with them both. It was probably his idea to target Dedei as revenge for the Tony thing. I thought about hiding their bodies but it wouldn't have worked that way. Their bodies needed to be found.' I say rubbing my wrists. 'Mossi was nothing. He was a tour guide at best. I wanted to meet the one they called boss... the men who would be snatching them and transporting them... I killed them and went home and waited for that call.'

I think I hear the sound of a gun being fired from within the shipping container and if it is gunfire I wonder how much of it is being picked up by the police if the battery hasn't died.

'Yeah. He did.' I nod, 'And they all showed up.'

'They called didn't they?' Klu says.

I'm about to ask Klu if he can tell whether somebody's trying the door when the police appear and there are lights everywhere.

The police must be monitoring the signal from Fitz's phone as they go straight to the container.

Three officers jump out of the first car, two from the second. The lights from their new walkie-talkie screens shine as they run to the container holding Mossi, Togolese Mike and all the goodies.

Suddenly the officers pull back, two of them staying close enough to size up the container and maybe to hear with difficulty what is going on inside. One, bending over, creeps towards it and examines the phones lying near the container.

He throws himself on the ground. Someone has shot or is firing at the container's locks and surrounding area. The officer on the ground stays down, then considering the place unsafe drags himself off towards the bright cars on his hands and elbows, like a fast-moving tortoise.

The police officers probably couldn't have unlocked the container if they'd wanted to, which they no longer do. They've withdrawn and are shouting at each other and at the man or men in the shipping container. If the combat police weren't readying themselves before, they are now.

'Look at them bitches running and hiding and waiting for the real police!' said Klu, before asking, 'You get this from Tony too?'

'Yeah.'

The police are still doing nothing and I can't see any activity from the container.

'These two girls that used to work at your mum's restaurant, they were working with the Albanians sending them women to wherever.'

'And they took Fanny's son,' I breathe.

'Your Fanny?'

I nod. 'He disappeared months ago. I didn't think anything of it 'cos he wasn't in the game. It took me this long to work it out.'

'Oh shit! They fucked up!'

'Did he know?'

'No but Fanny's brother does now.'

'You told him?'

'No. Mossi did. Back in Camden I called him and had Mossi explain everything, before he went into the boot.'

A police wagon arrives and ten to a dozen officers pour out of the back. Maintaining a twenty foot perimeter around the container behind vehicles and safe angles, the armed police surround the car probably shouting freeze and other such commands.

The car reverses out of sight but is soon back and this time, fucked-up beyond all recognition as it forces its way through. The police marksmen fire warning shots. There are sounds of metal hitting metal where bullets ricochet off the ground. It's then I start seeing smoke. I stand and move back to a hiding place from where I can see less but which makes for an easier getaway. It will soon be time for us to leave.

'Shit!' Klu shouts before he can stop himself. 'This is some movie shit!'

The police inch towards the quietly smoking shipping container. One of them is very familiar.

'Did you leave your ID and that in there?' Klu asks.

'Nawh, I shake my head. 'That's for faking your death. I don't want them to think I'm dead. My car's enough, I want them to know they were trying to set me up. Everything else will point elsewhere.' I watch the efficient walk of D. I. George and wonder what's going through her mind as she picks up the R. M. Laylor pen drive next to the phone that summoned her and her people.

I feel uneasy now. The police and fire services are going to be busy here for the next few hours. There's bound to be some uniforms taking a look around. 'We should probably get going.'

Behind us I can hear fire engines, ambulances, and the sound of police sirens. Klu and I make good time walking to where his stolen motorbike is conspicuously covered with a twenty-metre wide tarpaulin. It's then we hear a loud bang which makes everything shake.

Either my car has exploded with either Togolese Mike or Mossi inside or one of them got my car started and rammed it through the front of that shipping container. It didn't matter. Klu and I would soon be gone.

'You've got blood on your pretty suit mehn,' Klu says looking at me.

I look in a duffel bag of things I took from my boot before putting Mossi in. Alongside my criminal toolkit, missing binoculars and three cartons of pineapple juice, are jeans that look good with Mossi's black city coat. I replace the bloody shirt with a collarless one.

I ask a question I've been asking all my sleep-deprived day. But now, for the first time of asking I expect an answer or I won't be responsible for my actions.

'Klu, where's Buki?'

'I took her to mum's house. I told mum The Key had one of those urban celebrity substance abuse problems and she shouldn't let her leave... and you know what mum's like!'

I throw the bag over my shoulder. I take a special look at the motorbike I'm about to be passenger on for the first time. It's a red bike with a lot of metallic numbers on the main bit behind the handlebars. I still don't know much about motorbikes but I can tell this one is fast.

'Where'd you get this bike from?'

'Took it off a nigga!' Klu allows me to take the seat on the bike behind him.

Tribal leaders in the Sudan don't take cheques!

It's a complicated maze that leads to Aunty Merley's house. The house is exactly like it always looks. As usual, I'm reminded of the first time I was brought here. The smells take me back to being a fourteen-year-old boy. I hadn't thought I would get a mum any more. Then Aunty Merley found me.

I knock on the door.

It's the first time I've known exactly where Buki Nneka is and almost exactly what she's doing. Aunty Merley will have her doing chores or reading the Bible.

'Hello Aunty Merley,' I say when she opens the door.

'Nii Nathan,' she nods back. Cautious, then sure, she motions me inside.

Buki Nneka, hugging herself appears next to the older woman who could be her mother. Aunty Merley could be mother to all of us.

I remember how I had felt the first time I saw Aunty Merley. I tried to prevent myself from feeling that way, I had thought I was beyond hoping, but not so. I don't smile at Buki Nneka and she doesn't smile at me. She eyes me up and down. Maybe she is still scared. I don't say anything now. I notice how smooth her skin is. A woman whose life has been as rough as hers has no business with such smooth skin. I feel bad for manhandling her at the club and for every time she's been mistreated during her whole life.

Aunty Merley looks up at me and folds her arms with that look that says just because I am bigger than her I shouldn't get the wrong idea.

'I hear that a friend of yours helped you to talk to the mayor to keep the park open.'

'Something like that,' I nod.

She nods and then she's not frowning as much, 'You're a good boy. Remember that okay. Don't let any of them tell you different.'

She stops saying nice things so Buki Nneka doesn't hear. She has her extravagant cloak and hood jacket zipped up so that she looks more traditional, safer. She hugs it close around her over a pair of Dedei's more sensible jeans.

'Come on, let's go,' I say.

I hear her say thank you to Aunty Merley. I follow Buki as she walks down the street not looking back at me.

We walk side by side, close. I'm tired and I don't know what to say to her. She knows what I am. It's not hard to tell.

I want her and I don't know why. I don't like not knowing why I'm doing something or not doing something. I don't know when I decided not to give her to Fielding. In not handing her over I'd just be another man she's worked her stuff on. But I want her. I'm just like every man she's ever known since she got here or even before.

'I saw you,' she says breaking the silence.

I look at her.

After a few seconds I choose as a reply, 'When?' and not 'Where,' because I think I already know the answer to both.

'Does Grayson want to kill me?'

'Yes,' I give her the short answer.

'I knew it when he didn't want me to go out today. Like he cared where I went or if I got hurt today. He never did before, so I knew something was wrong.'

There was another pause.

'Grayson was everywhere in the bad things everybody was doing, and he tried to make me a part of it too. I didn't understand why he did such things, he didn't need the money but he enjoyed it. Why, I don't know.'

'You know why,' I say. 'It's about power and being in control. He was the commanding officer directing operations.'

'I found some papers with his company's picture on them. The way he reacted I knew there was something wrong. I wanted to throw them away... or hide them somewhere.' She pauses. 'Somewhere even Grayson Fielding wouldn't find them, and I could forget about them.'

She couldn't. Fielding had known about her workshop and sent his useless bastard son number two and he had found out about the lawyers and sent his useless bastard son number one. Today was the day Grayson Fielding had chosen to try and use me to help him get rid of all the people engaged in a particular kind of crime... to leave the field wide open.

'I just wanted to be rich and famous! I thought I did.' Buki cries fully now, holding nothing back. She throws her arms around me and hugs me.

'Mossi, Patrick Fitz, how did it all start?' I ask.

'We met in Cromber's club, the one in east London,'

Buki tells me the story of my day and I'm glad she's holding me and I'm holding her too so I can't see her eyes. I don't need to see Buki lie or whatever it is she does to men to confuse them.

Buki breaks off the embrace but holds both my hands in hers. She's a beautiful liar surrounded by bigger liars but enough of it is true. I'm overwhelmed by her smell. She smells like purity. If ambition and determination were a woman, that woman would be Buki. Only her conscience held her back.

'Angelica and Lavinia wanted me to work for them. Finding girls, Black girls, Africans to be slaves... slaves for sex. When they tried, the Black girls asked too many questions or their families got in the way.'

Buki continues with her voice becoming a whisper and I think of Dedei. Klu is across the road leaning on the motorbike.

'They have places where they would get them hooked on drugs so they wouldn't remember anything, and places to take them where women can't go to the police. They would give me five thousand for every woman I found for them...'

I don't say anything.

A silver BMW appears.

'Why did you help me?' She looks like she wants to cry again. The glitter around her beautiful eyes makes it look like she's been crying for a long time.

I tell her.

'My mother... you're like her.'

'That wasn't her was it?' Buki asks.

There's a long pause and then I say, 'No... Not Aunty Merley. I never knew my mother. When I saw your picture yesterday you looked how I imagined she might have done.'

'I've never reminded anybody of their mother before. Should I say thank you for that?'

'Maybe I'm supposed to thank you.'

I had never thanked Aunty Merley. I had never known how to thank her because then I didn't think of my mother as often, and how she had gone missing. And why. Inside the car is Armah, his girlfriend and his driver-bodyguard. In Ghana, where I'm sending her, Armah is famous, like Buki had been famous here.

'That's a guy I know. A friend – he can get you where you'll be safe, in Ghana.'

'In Ghana?' Buki is taken aback, 'How long do I have to stay there?'

'For as long as you need to... You can stay out of sight... but loads of expats are going back these days and everybody but me is on Facebook and Twitter, so you'll be recognised and all over the internet by this time tomorrow.

Armah pushes the passenger door open.

Buki smiles sadly, 'Can't I stay with you?'

The halo headlights continue to shine spotlights on us. I hand Buki the blue box from the black and white house. Buki holds the box.

'By the time I went to school my mother would already have gone to one of her jobs, so she would put my money for the day in a box for me... most mornings.'

I think of the innocence contained in the suitcase.

'That suitcase it was in. I can send it on to you.'

Buki looked thoughtful. 'That house is a crime scene now?'

'Yeah, but there are ways around that.'

She half-nods. 'No, but look after it for me.' She passes me a left luggage ticket from Euston Station. 'The company papers are there.' The papers will be something of hers I can keep. Something real, her late and valuable contribution to my search for her. I look around and see that Klu is talking to Armah. Kuvodu, the bodyguard, hasn't left the driver's seat but watches everything.

Genevieve sees the opening and talks to Buki, 'My mother and I are fans of yours!'

Buki beams and a friendship starts between two beautiful Black women that should last the flight.

'Awula kēkē?' Armah asks me.

'Just the girl.' I help Buki into a back seat after he's done the same for Genevieve.

'Good!'

I think Armah's grateful. He wants to see how long I'll stay alive for or he doesn't want the competition in Ghana.

'Thanks... Benjamin,' I say.

'Call me Kob, man!'

With the two men in the front and the two women in the back, the big car rolls away. Their exit wants to be poignant but I know that undignified queues and plastic seats await them before an uncomfortable and long flight.

It's not fair that she's going to Ghana when I might just belong there. It's a country my mother might have been from and I might belong to but for her it was just any country that will be a refuge.

'It breaks your heart.'

'That depends if you have a heart though, doesn't it?'

'It don't break your heart, huh?'

'No.'

'But it would have. I don't think I really have a heart. I've got the thing that pumps the blood around my body but not what people mean when they talk about their heart getting broken.'

'I thought not. It's lucky you met my mum and us. You could have been a straight-for-hire killer, or a soldier or even a policeman bluhd!' Klu pauses to make sure being compared to a policeman doesn't send me into the sort of maniacal rage he would go into if I did the same to him. 'Is her heart broken do you think?'

'She's from Darfur man. If her heart hasn't been fully broken by now, something from the thirtieth floor of a London penthouse building won't do it.'

'You know...' Klu scratches his beard, 'It's one of them legends come true! Buki Nneka is the face of hustle. Mossi was the one who had her locked up or your studio boy. Cromber tried to save her. But he crapped out. Fitz thought he was in charge but your Mr Fielding is really the one earning!' Klu spits, 'That's Cameroon behaviour!'

A pause then I have to ask, 'What the fuck is Cameroon behaviour??'

'Cameroon? Nigeria? They share a border innit! It's some fraudulent shit. Geddit? Laugh now and figure it out later, bruv! Your geography teacher died a long time ago Challey!' Klu says with an exaggerated African accent. 'Fielding sent his sons against us! Against Adjei and Mensah! Chiaa!' After a pause Klu finally makes his point. 'He practically killed his own sons.'

With the jeans, quiet designer black trainers and Mossi's three-quarter-length coat, I really do look overly like an east London criminal. There's no helping that. Sometimes, you have to look what you are.

'This is for Dedei,' I dangle the keys for Mossi's Bentley and I tell Klu, 'I'll take the bike.'

Klu tells me, 'Feel free!'

This gangster heads west on the red motorbike.

Dying is never good for business...

I had been wrong when I said the Albanians weren't interested in empire building. The Albanians were just different kinds of empire builders. They'd been empire builders for hire. Fitz had thought a lot of things, like a small boy believing everything his father told him. He thought those Albanians worked for him but while they were killing Cromber for Mossi they were killing his brother for Fielding. Kidnapping me had been sloppy but didn't necessarily get in the way of Fielding's plans for me, like they did.

I was standing outside a house in The Bishop's Avenue owned by a man that had tried to get me killed. He had sent me on a wild goose chase, leaving dead bodies wherever I went. He knows I would die rather than go to prison and last night I was supposed to die. Then again, maybe he had paid me the greatest compliment I've ever received. He had set me up with the police, African and Albanian gangsters and his crazy sons.

I repaid him in kind by killing one of his sons. I put in the code Grayson Fielding had given me and the security gates open. I rev the motorbike as hard as I can and accelerate. I notice the helicopter towards my right. Ten metres before the house I veer off towards the side and jump off. There's a sound of solid glass breaking as the sliding motorbike smashes through the glass panelling of the French windows.

Criminal Damage Without lawful excuse: 2 counts
Maximum Penalty: 10 years imprisonment
Criminal Damage Act 1971, section 1

I run up to where the motorbike has made a hole, big enough for me and my army to enter. Instead of alarms, there's the sounds of footsteps coming towards me and three voices. Quickly getting myself into the house I ready my gun.

GRAYSON FIELDING CALLING...

I had expected this. Quickly I flip my visor up to take the call from my hands-free gadget and flip it back down. The security guards find me very quickly and a big grey-suited man grabs at my gun hand. I hear Fielding's voice and I fancy these security men can hear him too in the grey coiled earpieces reaching downwards around their spines. I try not to panic, knowing this fight for my gun is going to be different from any of the encounters I've had so far. There will be none of Mossi's sloppiness nor Togolese Mike's excess facial hair to grab hold of as Fielding's men are pure muscle and discipline. I find myself jumping through the air to save my arm from being broken, aware of Fielding's voice in the background.

I land on the floor and before the three men can be on me again I shoot haphazardly at toe level. Two shout and, only one falls and two back off with their hands raised.

It's cowardly to shoot at unarmed men but there's three of them, so I do. I'm tired and I need them quiet.

Assault occasioning actual bodily harm: 3 counts
Maximum Penalty: Three years Imprisonment
Offences Against the Person Act s47

I pull out six of the hardest plastic ties and get to work tying up Fielding's in-house security team. I make sure the ties binding the three men's wrists and ankles feel like they'll hold for at least ten minutes. All the time Fielding is talking to me but I don't hear what he is saying. He seems to be talking about a painting on the wall. We hear the sounds of a door or doors opening and footsteps. It doesn't sound like more bodyguards to be locked in the panic room...

'I didn't expect the day to turn out quite like it has...' Grayson Fielding's voice tails off as I approach him, my shoes creaking on the parquet floor. 'That wouldn't happen to be one of my guns would it?' he asks my helmet. 'It was your misappropriation of my property that made me aware of you.'

I ease the visor away from my eyes but not removing the helmet. I keep my gun on him all the while looking for anybody else who might be in the house. I don't want any witnesses to what is about to happen.

'Employing you to look for my wife meant I knew where you were.' After a pause he adds. 'Where is she by the way?'

I take the helmet off, before replying. 'She's not coming back.'

'That wasn't what I paid you to do, was it?' Fielding sounds to me like somebody asking a rhetorical question. He put the grey car on me and has probably never trusted anyone, from his sons on down. Indeed we both know the other half of that two hundred and fifty thousand pounds won't be coming with me this morning.

'This is what you want.' I hand him the left luggage office ticket. 'When you get the contents of the box you will have the documentation that will link you to a mob of murdering Albanians and your business sidelines of gunrunning and people trafficking. You set me up to be the fall guy for all the killings you ordered in the last twenty-four hours and then have me killed when I was of no further use.'

'That was Roacher's idea. It would have made everything very neat and tidy. Roacher has always been a disappointment to me both in the army and since, so I should not be surprised things went wrong. You've had quite a day.'

'That's what your son said before I shot him. He had quite a day too.'

'Patrick and his brother were even greater disappointments to me. I made a mistake with their mothers so I suppose I was at fault. I always had a weakness for lower-class women. A bad habit I picked up in the Army.'

I check my watch, and wait.

'My Buki saw you,' Fielding says nonchalantly, changing the subject.

I think of Buki's face when she first saw me in the club and when she had said, 'I saw you.'

'You know don't you? She saw you kill and you still let her go.'

The footsteps are closer now and soon the room is full of Turks. They are all wearing leather jackets and leather gloves but no masks.

Fielding exhales and looks at the men, then at me.

'These gentlemen are not the police I take it? Going to the

police is not your style is it?

'No. And you're above the law aren't you?' I say to Fielding. 'This is a friend of mine. It was his brother you killed and his nephew your east-European workforce kidnapped. I called him earlier and had Mossi explain everything. I don't know what he's going to do to you. I don't want to know. Maybe you've got enough money to pay him off. I don't have children but I hear they're supposed to be priceless to their parents and relatives.'

The Turks carry tools and cutting implements I've never seen before.They were probably used for farming a century ago but not in this country. Fielding is about to do the finest negotiation of his life. They ask me to leave with their eyes.

Fanny's brother looks at Fielding with dead eyes briefly stopping to look at me with a stern expression. 'If more Albanians come, they're yours okay.' He says so nobody knows who's doing who the favour.

I make a steering-wheel motion with my right hand at him. He nods and growls at one of his boys. 'Give him the keys for the Range Rover.'

I catch the key I'm thrown.

'I've been here a while. There might be a silent alarm... police...'

Fielding watches me leave, with an involuntary spasm of his neck, then his mouth, before he shouts, 'Wait Mensah! Your mother. I can find her. I can find whatever life she's leading wherever she is on the planet! I can find her. Don't let them do this! I can get the medical records of every woman in every city in the country. In every country!'

I look at Fielding. I think of all the people he's manipulated and controlled en route to their undoing and decide to go my own way, as usual.

'How long do you need for an alibi?' Fanny's brother asks.

'Give me twenty-five minutes.'

I take one last look at the mangled motorbike and the shattered glass it created.

Epilogue

'Thank you D. I. George for coming in specially to take my client's statement. I have a typed account made earlier today which Mr Mensah will sign at the end of the interview. It is the same account which I emailed you earlier. As I explained on the phone Mr Mensah was kidnapped yesterday by a gang of white thugs, blindfolded and taken to a basement location in central London where he was subject to physical intimidation which at times amounted to torture. While this was taking place someone arrived and there was an argument with his captors and a gun was fired. This altercation led to Mr Mensah's captors leaving the premises. Mr Mensah was eventually able to get free of his bonds and escape. Thinking his life was still at risk he went into hiding and informed members of his family in case they were in danger. It would seem that my client had been targeted by a criminal gang from eastern Europe who presumably had confused my client with someone else. Mr Mensah did not know any of his captors nor could he understand why he had been kidnapped. My client fears that his life is still in danger while these men are at large and so he must be very circumspect in his movements.'

D. I. George smiled and turned on the tape recorder. 'Interview with Mr Nathan Mensah at 10.45 pm on Tuesday...

present in the room Mr Mensah, his solicitor Monica Asere, D. I. George and P. C. Green…'

Glossary of Slang and Foreign Expressions

Aight – alright but in a hip and ghetto way (page 25)

Ahlie – okay? (page 135)

Awula kɛkɛ? – just the girl? (GĀ) (page 217)

Beshi – chill/hang out (GĀ) (page 125)

Betting-shop fly – a compulsive gambler who hangs about betting shops (page 161)

Bin – prison (page 31)

Black-Man's Wheels – a BMW (page 25)

Bly – rasta word meaning to get a favour or chance (page 9)

BM – baby mother (page 112)

Botoss – backside (page 108)

Buff – sexy (page 97)

Bumber – a term of exclamation and emphasis from Caribbean dance music (page 97)

Buss'N'Go – an improvised play on the shampoo brand 'Wash & Go'. Buss is a Caribbean term meaning to shoot or activate (page 204)

Challey – a term of endearment between Ghanaians (page 70)

Challeyland – Ghana (page 134)

Chelsea Tractors – a large four-wheel drive car (page 77–78)

Chiaa – the ghetto way of saying yeah (page 109)

227

Coyote – originally a person who smuggles immigrants into America (page 137)

Drum – cockney slang for place (page 25)

Fam/family – my friend (page 28)

Fefe ne efe – the name of a fela kuti song basically means beauty, specifically beauty of a woman (Twi) (page 131)

Fio – small (GĀ) (page 183)

Flip a bitch/Flippin' a bitch – an illegal Uturn (page 112)

Foomo – 'Behave!' (GĀ) (page 106)

FUBAR – Fucked Up Beyond All Recognition (US Marine Term) (page 187)

GARI – a popular West African food made from cassava tubers (page 94)

Gym monkeys – a person who spends all their time in the gym rather than going out (page 193)

Have a butcher's – to look at something (page 74)

Hēh! Mī ŋyē yē bīēē! – 'Hey! I'm walking here!' (GĀ) (page 89)

Hinky – strange (page 126)

Humble – a minor criminal offence (page 13)

Hundy – a hundred (page 121)

IC3 – Afro-Caribbean, in police terms (page 34)

Inna – nosy (page 8)

Jheeze – London term basically the same as OMG or Wow (page 25)

Juju – a term associated with witchcraft (page 126)

Knawmean? – you know what I mean? (page 32)

Mandem – a group of men or boys (page 73)

Mehn – man (page 112)

Naa Merley – the full name of the first-born female child in a family (page 106)

Nii Addy – the full name of the first-born male child in a

family (page 106)
Omoge – a beautiful woman (Yoruba) (page 132)
One shoe drops – American equivalent of the penny dropping/ understanding something for the first time (page 172)
One time – the police (page 57)
Oyinbo – a white person (Yoruba) (page 177)
Papa – big (GA) (page 183)
Pay-as-you-go-popos – retail or private security (page 33)
Pigeon – a female who goes out looking for dates (page 29)
Popo – a police officer (page 114)
Shisha bongs – hookah/ shisha pipe (page 89)
Shoot my cuffs – pull or jerk shirt cuffs out so they project over the cuffs of your coat (page 102)
Shottin' – dealing drugs (page 28)
Soundboys – reggae dancehall DJs (page 102)
Spark   punch someone in the face (page 33)
Stush – conceited, superior, having an air of bitchy hauteur particularly with regard to personal appearance (page 54)
To go see a horse about a dog – a remix of to see a man about a dog (page 70)
Trance music – a genre of electronic dance music that developed during the early 1990s (page 92)
Waste – inferior (page 128)
Weave – a form of hair extensions often used by Black women, and celebrites (page 188)
Weisse jungs bringen's nicht – white guys can't jump (German) (page 11)
Whip – car (page 197)
Widdit – with it (page 61)
Yardies – Jamaican-born gangsters (page 21)

Glossary

The page numbers in brackets refer to the first time an expression appears in the text.